A ZEBRA R...

MARI...

The Ghost and Mrs. Wenthaven

An unlikely pair was
headed for love...with
some otherworldly
help.

ZEBRA
U.S.$4.99
CAN $6.99

EAN

ISBN 0-8217-7237-6

9 780821 772379

5 0 4 9 9>

"Are you returning to London immediately?"

Dylan crossed his arms over his chest and gave her a knowing stare. "Are you eager to get rid of me?"

Cassie glanced away as a pang of guilt came over her. She decided to be frank. "Am I that easy to read?"

His lips curled at the corners. "An open book."

Heat rose in her cheeks. "I suppose a gambler is trained to see every nuance of his opponent's expression."

His smile broadened and he took a leisurely step toward her. "You're absolutely correct. I'm willing to bet you have a rather keen sense of observation yourself. However, it's not as attractive when accompanied by judgment."

She stood her ground as he kept coming closer, every step somehow a threat to her composure. "I've had nothing but sorrow and hardships in connection with gambling," she said, lifting her chin and staring straight at him. She could drown in those penetrating, beautiful blue-green eyes if she didn't take care, or be scorched by the powerful male allure he possessed.

He stopped right in front of her, his gaze following every contour and detail of her face. A small frown appeared between his eyebrows.

Her heart pounded, and her mouth felt suddenly dry.

"I think we'll get along just splendidly if you keep your comments to yourself, Cassie," he drawled. "I'm a little short in patience." As if pulled by a magnet, he swept her into his arms and caught her mouth in a sudden kiss that seared every inch of her being. . . .

<u>BOOK YOUR PLACE ON OUR WEBSITE</u> <u>AND MAKE THE</u> <u>READING CONNECTION!</u>

We've created a customized website just for our very special readers, where you can get the inside scoop on everything that's going on with Zebra, Pinnacle and Kensington books.

When you come online, you'll have the exciting opportunity to:

- View covers of upcoming books

- Read sample chapters

- Learn about our future publishing schedule (listed by publication month *and author*)

- Find out when your favorite authors will be visiting a city near you

- Search for and order backlist books from our online catalog

- Check out author bios and background information

- Send e-mail to your favorite authors

- Meet the Kensington staff online

- Join us in weekly chats with authors, readers and other guests

- Get writing guidelines

- AND MUCH MORE!

Visit our website at
http://www.kensingtonbooks.com

The Ghost and Mrs. Wenthaven

Maria Greene

ZEBRA BOOKS
Kensington Publishing Corp.
http://www.kensingtonbooks.com

ZEBRA BOOKS are published by

Kensington Publishing Corp.
850 Third Avenue
New York, NY 10022

Copyright © 2002 by Maria Greene

All rights reserved. No part of this book may be reproduced in any form or by any means without the prior written consent of the Publisher, excepting brief quotes used in reviews.

If you purchased this book without a cover you should be aware that this book is stolen property. It was reported as "unsold and destroyed" to the Publisher and neither the Author nor the Publisher has received any payment for this "stripped book."

All Kensington titles, imprints, and distributed lines are available at special quantity discounts for bulk purchases for sales promotion, premiums, fund-raising, educational or institutional use.

Special book excerpts or customized printings can also be created to fit specific needs. For details, write or phone the office of the Kensington Special Sales Manager: Kensington Publishing Corp., 850 Third Avenue, New York, NY 10022. Attn. Special Sales Department. Phone: 1-800-221-2647.

Zebra and the Z logo Reg. U.S. Pat. & TM Off.

First Printing: April 2002
10 9 8 7 6 5 4 3 2 1

Printed in the United States of America

*To my old friends
at Palm Harbor Natural Foods:
Elisa, Christie, Jenn L., Holly, John, Amy and
Bill, Mike, Chris, "Sunshine," Dianne, Emily,
Nick, Jason, Princess, Anna, Janay, Leslie,
Cyndi, Scott, Jenni, Jenn S., and Irene*

One

"Blasted landlubbers!" Captain Brooks spat and walked through the wall. "It was different in my youth; people had some sense then." He wiped a transparent hand across his brow.

When he thought he'd made some progress into the affairs of Fairweather, something always came along to ruin everything. If the letter, which he'd read while hovering over Mrs. Wenthaven's shoulder, was any indication, Fairweather would now fall into the hands of a useless wastrel, a member of the hopeless Wenthavens. After all the efforts he'd made to set things right, it was just too much to bear.

It had been different in the old days when men had some backbone and knew when to work and when to play.

From what Captain Brooks had heard, Dylan Wenthaven only knew how to play. It didn't bode well for Fairweather. The captain wafted an icy sigh into the room.

He glanced at the woman sitting by the table. His only hope was this admirable widow who had lived at Fairweather for seven months, Cassandra Wenthaven. Now there was a lady any man would be proud to call his own! She might not have much in the way of superficial beauty, but she had a forth-right manner, a heart of gold, and a level head on her shoulders. Fortunately, her disastrous marriage to that other Wenthaven mealworm, James, hadn't ruined her backbone. Without a doubt, it was as solid as the day she was born.

She did have very beautiful eyes. They were large and expressive, warm and gold-brown, eyes that made a gentleman feel good—even if she did see right through him.

Mrs. Wenthaven had only one unfortunate trait—she didn't believe in ghosts.

Cassie crumpled the letter with a gesture of disgust. "We're in duty bound to inform you of the recent transference of ownership of the Fairweather estate to Mr. Dylan Wenthaven, and that you can no longer reside . . ." she recited aloud and tossed the paper ball into the basket on the floor.

So that was the lay of the land. Dylan Wenthaven, James's younger brother, was to bring a waft of dissipation to this house. Darn it all, the Wenthavens had brought enough heartache to last her a lifetime—James most recently. And now she had to suffer an encounter with Dylan. He was the worst scoundrel of the lot, according to rumors that had been circulating since his twin brother, Dermott, had died in a riding accident.

Rufus Wenthaven, the Earl of Seffington and James's grandfather, had offered her refuge at Fairweather when she'd discovered that James had gambled away all his prospects then gone off to fight the French in Spain, only to die in the first battle.

That should have been the last of her dealings with the Wenthavens, but no. Evidently she hadn't suffered enough.

Cassie adjusted the lace-edged high collar of her lavender gown. James hadn't been worth mourning for, but she'd spent six dutiful months in black, and she couldn't wait to wear something more striking, even if society dictated a full year for deep mourning. Not that she could afford any new gowns right now . . . possibly a few bright ribbons.

She sighed and touched the back of her neck. A cold draft had lifted the tendrils there for a moment. This old heap of stones had more cracks than a dried mud puddle, but she was quite fond of Fairweather. It had character, just like a person.

Many, many generations of the colorful Brooks family had lived and died within these walls. All had left something of themselves behind, creating an atmosphere that kept insinuating itself under her skin.

She disliked the thought of having to leave Sussex and Fairweather. She disliked even more the thought of welcoming Dylan Wenthaven to its portals. But maybe he wouldn't stay long after he heard the proposition she had to offer.

She tucked the stray tendrils of hair under her modest white cap and went to the window. Beyond the overgrown grounds, the Channel held the deep blue of the summer sky, and the wind made brilliant sparkles of light on water. She loved the view of the sun playing over the sea, always inspiring and uplifting.

If Dylan didn't like her proposal, it would be dif-

ficult to find a lovely vista like this again, she
thought with a sigh of regret.

Lord Seffington must have been about in his head
when he deeded over the estate to Dylan, even
though Dylan's mother had been a Brooks. The oldest cousin, Thomas, would have been the better
choice, but he'd inherit the Seffington title and all
that went with it.

Dylan would not be happy to learn the sad state
of his inheritance, and maybe that would play in her
favor.

At dawn the following morning, Dylan pulled in
the reins of his horse at the outskirts of Fairweather's
weed-and-sapling-filled park. Mist hovered over the
ground, making the scene seem unreal. Someone had
scythed a path up to the back door, but otherwise
the grass grew knee high, and profuse vines rambled
up the sides of the mansion's crumbling stone walls
and spilled over the roof. The house was as he remembered, the half-timbered main part built in the
seventeenth century, the rambling additions made
from brick and local stone. His mother had grown
up here—a happy childhood, no doubt.

Dylan rubbed his gritty eyes, but that only made
them worse. He'd stayed up longer than he'd antici-
pated, and now his head pounded from the afteref-
fects of the brandy he'd consumed the previous
evening. He should have stayed at the inn to sleep
it off, but he was eager to see his mother's old estate,
which he hadn't visited since he was a young boy.
Now he nearly regretted coming here.

According to Seffington, his miserly grandfather,

the Brooks family had been a flighty and irresponsible lot. They had fallen into the trap of borrowing money from Seffington, who'd eagerly taken the deed to Fairweather when they failed to repay the loan. However, the old bleater hadn't seen his way to pay for its upkeep. Fairweather was not much more than a ruin.

"Damn it all!" Dylan closed his eyes and pinched the bridge of his nose. His headache was increasing by the minute. A strong cup of coffee laced with brandy would be just the thing.

Joker, his tawny gelding, moved restlessly under him, as if feeling his owner's pain.

"Grandfather must be chuckling in his grave for playing such a nasty trick on me," Dylan said aloud. He clenched his jaw in anger and snapped the reins. He might as well find out the whole of it, or turn around now and never come back.

Something propelled him forward. He thought for a moment of his mother, who'd died when he was five. She would have liked him to live here, where they had spent many happy moments. He remembered picking tiny crabs in the cove below the estate when the tide was out.

He tied Joker to a tree, then waded through the grass to the front door. Even from a distance, he noticed that the wood panels had warped, and he had to tug hard to open the door. He wasn't surprised to find it unlocked. The hinges creaked hideously. No butler here to greet a body.

A musty smell met him in the hallway, as if the house had not been aired out for a long time. But that was not true. He could see the misty outdoors through cracks on both sides of the windows. Filled with misgiving, he took a few steps along the moldering red carpet that had holes as big as the moon in two places.

To his left, the door to the parlor stood open, revealing shabby furniture. To his right were doors to the library, another parlor, and the morning room.

"Hello? Anyone here?" Dylan shouted. The atmosphere seemed to absorb his words as if they had never been spoken. It was as if he'd entered a strange place with a different heartbeat than the rest of the world.

He heard sounds of movement from the back of the house. An old man dressed in tatters of various shades of gray ambled into the hallway. He lifted a lit candle to peer closely at Dylan. Wisps of white hair hung under a knit cap that had unraveled along the edge. A piece of yarn curled over the man's furrowed forehead, but his blue eyes were keen amid the folds of wrinkled flesh.

"Mighty early for a visit, ain't it?" the old man said suspiciously. "Mrs. Wenthaven ain't up yet, and the Elderberry sisters went off on their early morning walk. Mrs. Granger is putting the coffeepot on the fire. Who are ye?"

"I'm the new owner, Dylan Wenthaven."

The old man's eyes popped. "No, ye never! Ye sure have growed since I last clapped eyes on ye. Haven't shown yer nose in these parts for a long time. I'll have to tell Mrs. Granger ye've arrived. We knew ye were comin', but not when."

"And who are you?" Dylan asked, his words halting the man's retreat toward the kitchen.

"Ned Biggins, sir. I've worked here all me life,

and knew ye when ye were in shortcoats. A right scamp ye were, too, as was yer twin."

"Sorry, but I don't remember you. Fairweather has changed a lot since I was a boy."

"Th' old place has come into its last years, just like meself," Ned said. " 'Tis rather sad, ain't it? Once it was a grand old beauty, with proud pillars at the front and marble terraces at the back. Nothing but rubble left, alas. The very brick walls are coming apart, sir. They *are* ancient, of course, but one would like to think they'd have a bit more life in 'em. But wi'out upkeep . . ." His voice drifted off.

Dylan clenched his fists at his sides as the truth seeped into every corner of his being. He could never live here. He had no funds to put into bricks, new timber, and necessary repairs. As a matter of fact, he had about a hundred pounds in his saddlebag, and Edward Bunney owed him two hundred.

If luck ran his way soon at the gaming tables, he would be plump in the pocket, but would there ever be enough? Gambling was what supported him, and he was usually blessed with great luck, but could he win enough for these repairs? He would have to win a huge sum of money.

He could always sell the land.

"Yer mother would be ever so sad if she thought ye would get rid of the family home," Ned said with a disapproving frown. "She loved it here. The Brooks family always thought the world of this place."

Did he read my thoughts? Dylan wondered, startled, but Ned gave no indication he'd listened to Dylan's mind. He finished his amble toward the back, where a door led to a narrow corridor.

"I'll tell Mrs. Granger ye'll be wantin' breakfast. Fresh eggs we have, bread, and a slab of ham."

Dylan nodded, his stomach rebelling at the thought of food. What he needed was some sleep. He glanced up the stairs, noting the threadbare carpet and the dust on the carved balustrade.

To his surprise, a woman stared at him from the landing above. Her level brown gaze bored straight into his soul for a moment, and he swallowed hard. It captivated him like nothing had for a long time.

Cassie. He hadn't seen her since her wedding. Then she'd appeared an innocent tender flower. That had now been replaced by striking womanhood. There was nothing weak or tender about her now, only strength and purpose, an allure all her own.

Her hair, which he remembered to be an unusual brown-gold, was covered with a large plain mobcap, and a high-necked white nightgown and robe clothed her body. Her face was thin—mayhap a trifle too thin—with high cheekbones and arching peremptory eyebrows. Her lips looked tight, as if she'd already judged him and found him lacking.

"We didn't expect you so soon," she said coolly.

He held her unblinking stare, his whole body taut. "Cassie, it's been a long time. Aren't you pleased to see me?" Dylan tried to smile, but her cool demeanor stopped any attempt at pleasantries. He leaned one elbow on the balustrade and fastened his gaze on the vaguely rounded form of her body under the voluminous robe. "By the way, what *are* you doing here, Cassie?"

"Lord Seffington's solicitor must've informed you about my presence. I've been living here since James died, and I know everything about the estate."

He smiled indulgently. "Everything?"

He noticed her hands clenching around the top railing, and her voice held an arctic edge. "Mr. Wenthaven, I have a proposal that might benefit both of us, but please let me make myself presentable first."

He quirked an eyebrow. "You look very charming as you are," he said, surprised that he meant it. He felt an inexplicable urge to look more deeply into those brown eyes and to fill his nose with the scent of her. His senses were playing tricks on him this early in the morning.

"Blandishments won't work on me," she replied haughtily. "I mean to speak business with you, sir."

He didn't look forward to talking business with a pinch-lipped widow so early in the morning. He glanced around the gloomy hallway. What kind of business could she offer? As far as he knew, she didn't have a feather to fly with.

"I think our business can wait until a later hour," he said. "I shall see you in the—my—library after breakfast."

For a moment he felt the satisfaction of ownership. Even if Fairweather was little more than a ruin, it was something solid, something he could call his own. It was a novel feeling, but Cassie's piercing brown gaze somehow reminded him of his shortcomings, as if she itched to take him to task for all the things he'd done wrong in life.

"We have a lot to talk about," she said and went back upstairs, her steps firm.

I doubt that, he thought. He walked across the hallway toward the library. What he needed was some coffee and a quiet moment to think things through, but it was not within his grasp. He came eye to eye with two tiny elderly women who wore decaying straw hats and faded hoop gowns that must have been fashionable fifty years ago. Identical pairs of blue eyes stared at him curiously.

He bowed stiffly. "Dylan Wenthaven at your service. And who might you ladies be?"

He noticed immediately that they were twins, and the dreaded churning pain in his heart he'd fought every day since Dermott died came back. His twin, his mirror. He took a deep, steadying breath.

One of the ladies pursed her wrinkled mouth and tilted her head to the side. "I'm Hazel Elderberry and this is my sister, Hermione. We live here. You're the young man who's come to turn all of our lives upside down."

"You *what?*" He glanced from one to the other, noting that they didn't look particularly perturbed.

They nodded. "Yes. Cassie, who is the kindest of souls took us in when we didn't have anywhere to go. And now you plan to throw us out." She tilted her head to the other side. "What do you think, Hermione? Is he a beast?"

"I don't know," Hermione said timidly.

Hazel's laughter chased away the shadows in the room. He noticed she had a wart on her chin. By that, he could easily tell them apart. "My dear, methinks he's a hero in the making. After all, he has a gargantuan task ahead of him, and we can surely help. Sir, I don't think you can do without us as things stand around here."

Dylan felt slightly dizzy. "Help?"

"Trust us," they said in unison and stepped through the door to the front parlor. "We're very handy with needle and thread."

Dylan had the craziest picture of them sewing bricks together with red silk. A strong urge to escape came over him, but he set his jaw and walked into the library.

Cassie dressed in one of her lavender gowns with a matching spencer to protect her from the chill of the early morning. She pinned up her long curls into a chignon and covered her tresses with a frilly cap.

Dylan was just as she remembered—strikingly handsome, with dark brown wavy hair, blue-green eyes in a well-proportioned face with a strong jaw and prominent nose, broad shoulders, and splendid long legs. His virile form, elegantly dressed in buckskins and a blue coat, was a disturbing sight to any female heart, but she scoffed at such weakness. Anyone could tell by his haunted gaze that he'd spent the night staring deeply into one bottle or another. Probably gambling as well. She despised gamblers and drinkers. Vice ruined a marriage—something she'd experienced firsthand.

What if he didn't accept her plan? Fairweather had become her refuge, and she had no desire to find new accommodations for the time being.

She felt a breath of cold air on her neck and thought she heard a raspy voice whisper, "The house needs you."

Startled, she glanced around the room. No one was there but her. She must be more tired than she thought. Her nerves were playing tricks on her.

Putting her hand to her brow, she glanced at the pile of mending on the only chair in the room. Everything around her needed mending, and the thought brought her low for a moment. She straightened her back. It was never too late to improve conditions, no matter what state they were in.

She would have a cup of coffee and a slice of bread before confronting the man with the face of a fallen angel. It wouldn't do to approach business on an empty stomach.

Downstairs, she sped toward the kitchen before she would run into Dylan Wenthaven again. Fortunately, there was no sign of him.

The domestic regions had been added in the eighteenth century, a high-ceilinged stone building that jutted out at the back of the oldest part of Fairweather. Her heels clicked along the flagstones, and Mrs. Granger looked up from the skillet where ham sizzled. Merlin, the yellow striped tomcat, sat at her feet licking his chops.

"There ye are, dearie. I thought ye'd taken ill, but I see ye only slept later than usual."

Cassie shook her head. "No, I woke up when Mr. Wenthaven arrived."

Mrs. Granger's round face fell. She swept away the gray curls from her forehead with the back of her hand. "I do hope you can talk some sense into him. We can't have our lives upset by some old man's deathbed demands. You're as much a Wenthaven as he is."

Cassie smiled. "Your friendship warms me, but this is a legal issue."

Mrs. Granger poured a cup of coffee and set it before Cassie on the enormous, pitted oak table. Freshly baked currant buns sent out a delicious smell, and the cook pushed the basket toward Cassie.

"I made them special for ye, Mrs. Wenthaven. They're yer favorites."

Cassie nodded and took one. "I've tasted none better than these."

Mrs. Granger shrugged. "You're always so grateful and easy to please. Mr. Wenthaven seems the opposite, but I don't mind cooking for a handsome male for a change. Ned Biggins ain't much to look at. And mind you, he's too stubborn for me taste."

Cassie laughed. "He says the same about you. I think you two should make it a permanent union. If you do, I'll be at the wedding—if I'm invited."

Mrs. Granger swung a fork in a gesture of outrage. "Go on with ye! If Ned were the last male on earth, I wouldn't marry him. Ye're addlebrained to suggest such a thing, Mrs. W."

Cassie opened her mouth to defend her statement, but was interrupted by a loud wail at the back door. "What was that?"

"Sounded like a wee soul in pain," Mrs. Granger said. She set down her fork and opened the door. "Well, I never!"

"What is it?" Cassie joined the older woman who was bending over a basket.

"It's a young 'un."

Cassie stared at the small face peeping out of a threadbare blanket wrapped around a body that had tried to wiggle free.

Mrs. Granger bent from her plump waist with difficulty to hoist the basket into her arms. "There, there, love, don't cry," she crooned and set the basket on the table.

"Whose baby is it?"

"That I don't know, Mrs. W. No neighbors have

a little 'un that I know of. Look, it's a boy." Mrs.
Granger had unwrapped the blanket, and the baby
was naked except for a dirty white shirt.

"He's hungry," Cassie said, worried about the infant. "What in the world are we going to do about
him?"

"We'll have to notify the constable. Most likely
the mother couldn't keep him and thought this would
be a good place to leave him." Mrs. Granger clucked
her tongue. "How a mother could give up her child
like that is beyond me."

Cassie touched the head covered with light brown
silky hair. "How old do you think he is?"

Mrs. Granger lifted the crying baby into her arms.
"I'd say about eight months old. He reminds me of
the old days, when Granger and I had the boys."
Mrs. Granger's voice took on a sad tinge. "They be
long gone now. Sailed off on a ship headed for India
when they were sixteen and seventeen, never to be
heard from again."

"I didn't know that. I'm so sorry."

Mrs. Granger gave her a pleading glance. "No
matter what the new master says, ye can't leave now,
Mrs. W. I can't manage everything and this babe on
me own."

"You want to keep him?"

Mrs. Granger shook her head. "Oh no, but until
the authorities find the mother, we might as well care
for him. The orphanage is a foul place."

"I doubt Mr. Wenthaven would consider caring—"

The door to the corridor opened. Dylan stood on
the threshold, his hooded eyes taking in the scene.
"What's the commotion? I'm trying to get some rest,
but the wind whistles constantly in the window

cracks, and now an infant—" His eyes widened as he noticed the bundle in the cook's arms.

"Mr. Wenthaven," Mrs. Granger said briskly, "seems we've got a wee lodger. A sop of milk should quiet him nicely."

"A lodger?" Dylan's lips thinned, and Cassie expected him to explode. "What do you mean?" he asked in a quiet, menacing voice.

"Seems we—you—got appointed guardian by an unknown mother," Cassie said tartly. "Mayhap you already know something about it?" She was goading him, but there was always the chance he had fathered the babe on some poor wench. In all likelihood he had. Why else would a mother choose this decaying home to deposit her baby?

Cassie took in his stormy expression thoughtfully, then returned her gaze to the crying infant.

"Can't someone stop that caterwauling?" Dylan shouted. "It doesn't improve my headache."

"Your bellowing is giving the child a headache." Cassie frowned.

They stared at each other for a long moment that bristled with animosity—and something else. A dangerous fire crackled between them, and Cassie tore her gaze away. Just as she did, a pewter bowl fell from the mantelpiece and rolled across the floor to stop at her feet.

"Oh, me bowl wot Granger gave me on our tenth anniversary." Mrs. Granger handed the squalling baby to Cassie and bent to pick up the bowl. "He had a romantic heart, bless his soul."

"Things do seem to fall down a lot here—for no obvious reason," Cassie commented, cradling the infant.

"It's that surly old ghost, Captain Brooks. He likes

to play pranks," Mrs. Granger said with a sigh. She wiped the bowl with her apron. "Tosses things around and clumps about at night when a soul tries to get some rest. He's noisy but harmless."

"There are no ghosts," Cassie said.

"Captain Brooks?" Dylan asked, leaning both hands against the table as if too tired to hold himself upright. "The pirate who built this house in the seventeenth century?"

"Yes, the sailor in the portrait wot hangs in the library. He doesn't like arguments, so I'd keep my voice down if I were you," Mrs. Granger told Dylan, "or the captain might bring the roof down o'er yer head."

"It must be Ned walking about at night," Cassie said, finally managing to quiet the baby.

"No, ye heard the ghost, ye did. The captain likes the library the most; furniture moves and things disappear. I never go in there if I don't have to. Too cold and drafty for me old bones. Besides, I never like to be reminded of the hereafter."

Cassie shivered and glanced into the gloomy corners of the old kitchen. Who knew what lurked in places where the sunlight never reached? A ghostly hand seemed to move over her back, and she stepped closer to the hearth, where a bright fire glowed.

"Mrs. Granger, you're frightening Mrs. Wenthaven," Dylan drawled. His lips curved upward at the corners as Cassie sought the warmth, and she turned her shoulder toward him.

"Nonsense," Cassie said.

Mrs. Granger's voice was thoughtful. "If ye live here longer, ye will surely believe, Mrs. Wenthaven. I could tell you stories that'll make yer hair stand on end—"

"Another time," Cassie said hurriedly. Dylan laughed, and she threw an accusing glance at him. "I'm delighted you can enjoy yourself at my expense, Mr. Wenthaven. At least I know our encounter here at Fairweather has some purpose."

"Not that I've noticed," Dylan said, his face once again serious. A smile added much charm to his countenance, but now she focused on the lines of fatigue and overindulgence. She couldn't help but wonder if the baby would one day display a similar smile.

Mrs. Granger started warming milk for the infant, who lay quietly in Cassie's arms. Cassie noted in dismay that the child's eyes had a slightly downward slant at the outer corners, just like Dylan's, and the bold curve of his lips echoed those of the older man. It could be just a coincidence, but—

"I daresay you'll know what to do with the child for the time being. I shall contact the local constable and demand an investigation," Dylan said. "The babe shan't burden you for very long, Mrs. Granger."

"Oh, the wee one doesn't bother me," said the cook. "He adds a bit of life to this quiet corner. Fairweather could use some life after years of slumber."

"But not the kind of life Dylan Wenthaven will supply," Cassie said to herself. No one heard her. Anyway, it wasn't her place to tell the new owner what to do, not until he'd agreed on the deal.

"Look here," Mrs. Granger said, searching through the baby's basket. "A silver rattle."

Dylan took it and turned it in every direction. "It's a Wenthaven heirloom," he said, surprise in his voice. "How did that end up in the basket?"

"That's a very good question," Cassie said icily. "Mayhap the owner gave that as a gift to the baby's mother. I rather believe there's no mistake that we found the boy on *your* doorstep, Mr. Wenthaven."

He flashed her an angry glance. "I shall talk with you later."

Two

"You must see I'd be the perfect steward for this estate," Cassie said with more strength than she felt inside as she faced Dylan across the threadbare carpet in the library. "There's no reason you should have to bother with this place when you have no interest in it." She only assumed that fact, and she was surely bold to suggest it to him.

"I admit my mind is reeling. This turn of events has been somewhat sudden," he said. He looked at her for a long time, and she asked herself why her toes wanted to curl in the most curious fashion. His deep gaze did something to her insides, something warm and seductive. "Not that I have any intention of—"

"Pay attention, Mr. Wenthaven," she interrupted him without hesitation.

"You can at least call me Dylan," he said tiredly. "Why stand on formality?"

"Very well . . . Dylan. I've lived here for several months. I know what needs taking care of—"

"Taking care of?" His face took on an expression of outrage. "You wouldn't know where to begin, Cassie. The best thing to do would be to tear the buildings down and start over, or let it go to the highest

bidder. Mr. Duggan, the neighbor, approached me when he heard I'd inherited the place. He's been most insistent, almost menacing."

A sudden gust of wind moaned in the cracks around the windows. The air felt decidedly chilly, Cassie thought, and she pulled the fabric of her spencer more tightly around her neck. The ancient portrait of Captain Brooks hung over Dylan's head, its clear black gaze appearing to follow her every move. There was little resemblance between Brooks and the new owner. The harsh lines in Brooks's face made it easy to believe he'd lived a hard, adventurous life.

She looked at Dylan incredulously. "You would sell your mother's birthplace to strangers? Where is your sense of family tradition?"

He glanced away, his mouth hard. "Not much close family left now with both James and Dermott gone, and old Seffington."

"So much more important, then, to preserve what's left," she said. "If you allow me to stay on for the time being, I'll make sure you'll have a roof over your head for years to come. I'll oversee the repairs and make sure the workmen do a fine job. All you have to do is send me bank drafts from London to cover the costs."

"Drafts?" A shadow passed over his face. His broad shoulders stiffened, and he kept silent.

He doesn't have any accounts, she thought, visions of card tables with stacks of gold sovereigns flashing through her mind.

"You can think about it," she said coolly. "I helped Father in all his affairs, as I was the only child. I know how to run an establishment like this smoothly, even though there aren't any servants to speak of. We shall all have to assist."

"Except for you and Mrs. Granger, there's no one under eighty here." He walked toward her, his expression darkening with temper. "Now tell me, how did the Elderberrys end up under this roof? As far as I know, there has never been a connection between the Brookses and the Elderberrys."

"They are from my father's parish in Kent. I've known them all my life. They had absolutely nowhere to go after their father died. Whatever funds they possess have gone toward the upkeep here. If it weren't for the Elderberrys, there wouldn't be much in the way of coal and victuals. As you well know, James left me nothing but debts, and now with Seffington gone I'll have to look for permanent employment. Meanwhile, I'll do you the favor of looking after things here."

He gave the ceiling with its damp spots a thorough scrutiny. "Very well, you're hired—for now. But mind you, I'm in charge of every decision that concerns this place, and if I decide to sell, there's nothing you can do about it."

She gave a small nod of agreement as she sensed his determination. "Are you returning to London immediately?"

He crossed his arms over his chest and gave her a knowing stare. "Are you eager to get rid of me?"

She glanced away as a pang of guilt came over her. She decided to be frank. "Am I that easy to read?"

His lips curled at the corners. "An open book."

Heat rose in her cheeks. "I suppose a gambler is trained to see every nuance of his opponent's expression."

His smile broadened and he took a leisurely step toward her. "You're absolutely correct. I'm willing to bet you have a rather keen sense of observation yourself. However, it's not as attractive when accompanied by judgment."

She stood her ground as he kept coming closer, every step somehow a threat to her composure. "I've had nothing but sorrow and hardships in connection with gambling," she said, lifting her chin and staring straight at him. She could drown in those penetrating, beautiful blue-green eyes if she didn't take care, or be scorched by the powerful male allure he possessed.

He stopped right in front of her, his gaze following every contour and detail of her face. A small frown appeared between his eyebrows.

Her heart pounded, and her mouth felt suddenly dry.

"I think we'll get along just splendidly if you keep your comments to yourself, Cassie," he drawled. "I'm a little short in patience." As if pulled by a magnet, he swept her into his arms and caught her mouth in a sudden kiss that seared every inch of her being.

She stiffened and tried to push him away, but without success. For one shimmering moment of total delight, she melted.

His mouth left as abruptly as it had caught hers, and she could not find her breath until he released his hold on her. Her head spun, her thoughts in total disarray. She put a hand to her hair, finding her cap askew. With trembling fingers, she adjusted it and took a deep steadying breath.

His voice was raspy as he spoke. "I apologize. I understand you must be enraged by my behavior, but I just felt the damndest urge to kiss you."

"I guess you're used to acting on your 'urges,' " she replied, the steel in her voice belying the pounding of her heart. "Mind you, it won't happen again."

"I don't have much of a conscience."

She nodded curtly. "That doesn't surprise me in the least."

"But I'll do my best to keep my hands to myself."

"I'd expect no less. I shall speak with you later, when you've formulated some plans for the estate." Finding her legs unsteady, she walked out of the room. How could she ever look Dylan in the eye again and pretend nothing had happened between them?

Dylan watched her straight back as she left and sought for something that would keep her in his presence, but his mind was blank. A strange longing lodged in his heart, and the tension of the kiss kept him on edge as he walked out onto the crumbling terrace for some air. She had felt soft and strong at the same time, a wonderful handful of womanhood.

He dragged his hand across his forehead and walked to the weed-edged end of the terrace. In the distance, he saw a rider in the woods bordering the Brooks's estate with that of Julius Duggan. The portly shape in the saddle looked like Duggan himself.

Anger curled in the pit of Dylan's stomach as he remembered his last meeting with Duggan at one of the clubs in London. The old man had nothing but sarcastic remarks and sly innuendoes to impart about the ancient feud between the Brookses and the Duggans. Dylan had no interest in old feuds, and he wondered why Julius even bothered with keeping it up. There had never been an all-out war in his lifetime, but he remembered hearing about some duel between his grandfather and one of the Duggans in the last century. Dylan didn't really know how the feud had originated, but it had something to do with some ancient injustice done by a Brooks to a Duggan.

He saw the man riding closer. "Blast," he said under his breath, but decided a direct approach would be to his advantage.

He waded through the tall weeds to the edge of the garden—the only place that had been kept in perfect order. Straight rows of potato and cabbage plants grew in profusion.

"You have arrived to take stock, then," the older man greeted Dylan without as much as a bow of courtesy. His horse pawed the ground and tossed his head, but Julius Duggan kept him easily under control.

Dylan studied the hard, cold eyes set in a broad, fleshy face. No softening or neighborly cheer there, he thought. "Good morning to you, too, Mr. Duggan."

Duggan tilted his beaver hat forward to shield his eyes from the sun's glare. He gave Dylan a long, calculating look. "I don't expect any civilities from you, Wenthaven. None at all. In fact, it would appall me if you pretended we're good neighbors, as that's the furthest from the truth."

"I recognize your animosity, Duggan, but I have no intention of fanning any flames of hostility, nor will I bother to maintain ill will for something that happened long before we walked this earth."

Duggan's mouth parted in a small smile that sent a chill down Dylan's spine. "Be that as it may, I have come here to tell you once and for all that I intend to purchase this property and thereby wipe the slate clean." He made a dismissive gesture with his hand. "As it is, there's surely no reason for you to keep this heap of rubble."

"I don't do business with someone who professes an unjustified animosity toward me," Dylan said coldly. "I don't have any intention of selling Fairweather, but if I did, I would not consider your offer—not for any price."

Duggan swung his riding crop at a nearby tree branch, and his horse took a nervous step sideways. "You're a fool, Wenthaven! Let me inform you that no one will make you an offer for Fairweather, no one but *me*. And if someone did, I would make sure the deal went sour."

Dylan's anger boiled to the surface, but he kept his voice cool. "Is that a threat?"

"None of you will walk safely until Fairweather has become mine," Duggan shouted. His face twisted in a sneer. "The thatch of grass on which you stand should rightfully belong to me."

Dylan's voice grew ice-cold. "That's rubbish, and you know it! Bullying me will get you nowhere. If you as much as set your foot on my property again, Duggan, my retaliation will be swift and severe."

Duggan's glance measured him up and down. "You're making a mistake, Wenthaven. Don't play with me, or your lodgers will have to scramble to find a tombstone for your grave. I shall have restitution."

"You're more of a fool than I thought, then. Don't waste your energy." Dylan turned his back and went back to the heap that was his only real home. For a moment he felt a strange possessiveness, probably provoked by Duggan's abominable behavior.

"You'll come to a violent death like so many of

your ancestors," Duggan yelled after him. "Mark my words."

"Did no one ever tell you that charm will bring about desired results much faster than threats?" Dylan replied, annoyed but unperturbed by the verbal arrows. Duggan was nothing but a bag of hot wind.

He heard a series of curses behind him as he went back inside. Taken by surprise, he almost stumbled over the Elderberry twins standing behind the tattered curtains in the window. A spasm of the familiar pain of loss went through him as his own twin's face flashed before him.

He crossed his arms over his chest and glared down his nose at them. "Ladies, don't bother denying that you were spying on me and Mr. Duggan."

Hermione darted a nervous glance at her twin. Her chin wobbled slightly, and she squeezed the fat ginger cat in her arms.

Hazel's steady blue gaze held no fear whatsoever. "It pays to know what is transpiring around here," she said sharply. "You'd better pay attention, Mr. Wenthaven. That harum-scarum Mr. Duggan is up to treachery, and I suspect he won't give up his goal to take over Fairweather lock, stock, and barrel."

Dylan shrugged. "There's not much here to covet. He has many more acres and funds than he needs, and, as you well know, this house is barely an adequate shelter. Whatever grudge he holds is no business of mine. I had nothing to do with creating it."

Hazel poked a bony finger into his chest. "He's looking for *something,* and the search has only just begun. Don't tell me I didn't warn you."

Dylan smiled and grasped her dry, cool hand, then planted a gallant kiss on her fingers. "I appreciate your concern, Miss Elderberry, but I'm quite capable of taking care of myself and what's mine."

Hazel glanced at Hermione, her face registering censure. "He is a rogue, don't you think?"

Hermione nodded, smiling. The cat swished an annoyed tail and struggled to get down. "Merlin does not approve."

"Young man," Hazel continued, "your tactics are all good and well in a ballroom, but we have unfamiliar servants skulking around the grounds and ruffians riding on these estates snooping and carrying loaded pistols. I predict there's serious trouble ahead. As long as you were away, they could snoop unmolested, but—"

"Miss Elderberry, I appreciate your concern, but I've faced quite a few loaded pistols in my day, and they don't intimidate me."

"Irreverent as well," Hazel said to her twin. "A daredevil, I'd say. Won't have a long life."

Hermione nodded, allowing the cat to jump down, which he did with a yowl of displeasure.

"Mr. Wenthaven, we shall have to protect Cassie's heart as well. No rest for the weary, but we have our duty toward that kind woman. There's no way we can truly repay her for her goodness."

Dylan laughed. "So you judge me as untrustworthy?"

They both stared at him stonily.

"I suspect Cassie is quite capable of taking care of herself. It's unlikely she would fall for the Wenthaven charm twice."

"Pooh!" Storm clouds drew together on Hazel's brow. "James had no more charm than a toad. She was *forced* to marry that scoundrel." She paused, her gaze raking him from head to toe. "You, I fear, could wreak a lot of damage to that lady's heart. We shall see to it that it never happens. But if your intentions were honorable . . ." She let the words drift off and pulled her twin's arm. "Come along, Hermione. We have work to do." Hazel turned around at the door. "We shall keep a close eye on you."

Shaking his head in wonder, he watched as the ladies marched out of the room. He didn't know what he'd expected as a welcome to Fairweather, but surely he didn't deserve berating at every turn. All he'd done was to come home. *Home.*

He glanced around the dingy walls of the library, shivering as a sudden cold draft moved over him. He hadn't had a home for many years, not since his father died. He'd been floating from one lodging to the next in search of . . . something. Perhaps roots; he didn't know.

Three

Five days had passed and Dylan was still in residence. For some reason, it irked Cassie. How could she ever get started with any kind of improvements when he was hovering like that? He never settled down in any one spot in the house, except late at night when he brought out a brandy bottle. Nor did he appear able to decide when to take himself off to London.

A man of his ilk needed the glitter and the excitement of the capital, gaming tables and horse betting, something she didn't hesitate to point out every time she ran into him.

She caught him going through the attic on the morning of the third day, his face turned toward the rotting timbers of the roof. A serious frown marred his forehead, and his gaze was hard as he looked at her.

"Good morning," she greeted lightly, the memory of their kiss swimming unbidden to the surface of her mind. Because of that kiss, she'd tried to avoid him and had hoped he would take himself off. "I heard your footsteps and came to investigate. I see you've noticed the sad failures of the roof. When it rains—"

"It wouldn't be the first roof in England to be replaced," he snapped.

"I realize that," she replied coolly. "Perhaps your first decision should be about the roof."

He fastened all his attention on her, and again she had that curious feeling of her toes curling. She had to admit Dylan Wenthaven was not a weakling like James had been. There was nothing hesitant or spineless about him as he loomed over her, his gaze piercing.

"I assure you, Cassie, when I'm ready to make any kind of decision, you will not be kept in the dark. I understand your concern about the future of your shelter, but I'm quite capable of thinking for myself."

Her heart thudded wildly, and she had to look away from the intensity of his eyes. "I don't doubt that. However, I'm eager to start my new position as steward, and so far you've avoided giving me any kind of directions concerning your plans for the estate."

He smiled faintly. "I approve of your zeal. If you can find some workers to clear the grounds, that would be a good start. Also, I understand Mrs. Granger can't take care of the abandoned babe all on her own, so he will be part of your duties until we can find the parents."

She immensely disliked the slightly condescending tone of his voice. "Dylan, in all fairness, I'm doing you a favor by offering my help. It's undeniable that I have a greater understanding of the quirks and follies of the house."

"You have made that crystal clear to me, Cassie. I know I shall be eternally grateful to you as the work gets under way."

"Spare me the false courtesy." She glanced at him

narrowly, thinking of possible secret bank accounts or other financial supports that would pay for the restoration. "Then you intend to start the repairs?"

"As I said, you'll be the first to know about my plans," he said dismissively and brushed by her shoulder as he walked to the door that led down from the attic.

He didn't have to do that, she thought, clutching her hand to her heart. There'd been ample room to walk around her. His proximity had left her breathless. She glanced around the damp and gloomy attic space. It wouldn't do to have her senses touched by Dylan Wenthaven. It just wouldn't do.

Her thoughts in upheaval, she walked aimlessly among cobwebs and old moldering trunks that had been there for decades. An old coat hung in tatters beside a rotting stack of baskets. She had been through the attic once, but had never looked closely at any of the contents due to the deplorable conditions. Maybe this would be a project for a steward. A large bonfire behind the barn would welcome the rubbish littering the attic floor.

The swirling dust made her nose itch. She gingerly opened the lid of the nearest trunk, finding an ancient mouse nest and a stack of badly decomposed books. The fact that previous generations had let a small fortune in printed matter disintegrate surprised her. In her father's household, books had always been kept in pristine condition.

She lifted the spine of a volume as a violent sneeze overcame her. The printing on the first page intrigued her as she recognized the old-fashioned curlicues of a past century. These volumes were extremely old.

Another sneeze shook her, and she decided to investigate further at a later date. As she let the trunk lid fall, a mantle of icy-cold air enfolded her. How could it be so cold in the summer? she thought. A desire to open the trunk once more came over her, but she resisted the urge.

The old mice nests could wait a while longer, until she felt ready to tackle the decay. As she left, it was as if the cobwebs tried to entangle her and hold her back. Disturbed, she fled, closing the door behind her with force. A frisson ran down her spine, one she couldn't shake easily, even though she entered the brightly lit kitchen downstairs.

The baby squalled in his basket, and she lifted him up. The rosy-cheeked boy greeted her with a sudden smile, and she could not help but smile back. She thought he had the charming Wenthaven grin. Mrs. Granger, clearly out of breath, hastened through the back door.

"I had to get some herbs for the dinner stew," she said, "but I didn't want to leave the infant by himself. He let up a howl as soon as I set foot in the herb garden." She shook her head. "Has a healthy pair of lungs, he does."

"I would not be surprised if we found his father *near* Fairweather," Cassie said, noting again the Wenthaven trait about the babe's eyes. The thought annoyed her no end. First she had to take orders from a Wenthaven, and now she had to tend to—possibly—one of his illegitimate offspring. Life was never fair.

"You mean—" Mrs. Granger tossed her head in the direction of the inner house. Her eyes widened. "You'd niver—"

"Wouldn't surprise me," Cassie said, eying the gurgling child. "Bound to grow up into another rogue, as if the world wasn't filled with them already."

Mrs. Granger shook her head. "You sound too bitter by far for someone your age. Mark my words, there are decent men, and Mr. Granger was one of them. I have all the faith that ye'll find someone who appreciates yer virtues, Mrs. W."

"I'd have to replace one mobcap for another? It's highly unlikely I'll put myself under the commands of another husband, having escaped comparatively lightly so far. I'll not be some man's chattel again."

Mrs. Granger smiled indulgently. "I know you're a very capable woman, and I don't fear what would become of you, but the heart has a way of its own."

Cassie lifted the infant high into the air. "Here at Fairweather I'm unlikely to encounter any eligible gentlemen, which is just as well."

Mrs. Granger gave her a long, appraising look. "Be that as it may." She went over to the window, scanning the garden in the back. "Cassie, I have t'ask you this. When I gathered the herbs, I saw one of Mr. Duggan's servants running away from the house. Did he come on official business?"

"Not that I know of," Cassie replied, cradling the boy in her arms. "I didn't see anyone or speak to anyone, but I don't like it. You're not the only one who has seen trespassers."

"There's something afoot. 'Tis not the first time I've seen strangers snooping."

"As far as I know, there's nothing of interest, nothing to covet at Fairweather except the acreage itself and the protected cove on the beach."

"Old history, Mrs. W. I'd wager the Duggans know something we don't, and until we find out what they're looking for, we'll be kept in the dark."

"Hmmm. Why have they waited until now? Maybe I should have a little chat with Mr. Duggan. As steward of this estate, I have the right to know why he believes he can trespass on these grounds anytime he wants."

"Mrs. W., I don't trust Duggan. Never have, never will. I know he was involved in some unsavory dealings around here, even if the constables said otherwise. Duggan has no conscience, like the old pirate he is. He and that old sea horse Brooks were cut from the same cloth. Mr. Brooks can find no peace until—"

Cassie interrupted her. "Not that nonsense again! If you mention that old ghost story of Mr. Brooks walking these halls, I won't speak to you again."

Mrs. Granger raised her chin. "Very well, but there are some of us wot can 'see,' no mistake about it."

Cassie remembered the frisson following her from the attic, but dismissed it as feverish imagination. Dylan Wenthaven's presence was compromising her common sense, and she resented having her world invaded by some man whom she wasn't ready to call a gentleman by any standards.

Still carrying the baby, she said, "I'll have a word with Ned about the grounds. Before you know it, we'll have manicured lawns and flowers in the borders."

"Ye always were an optimist, Mrs. W. I shall keep ye in me prayers."

Cassie carried out her orders concerning the grounds, noting the morose look on Ned Biggins's face as he stared across the tall weeds running amok everywhere. She asked him to find some young sturdy boys to help him, but the look he gave her promised nothing but misery. Despite his attitude, the grounds *would* be taken care of, she told him in a voice that brooked no nonsense.

That battle launched, she set out to call on Mr. Duggan, her official business to explain the meaning of the word trespassing, only to be turned away at the door with the suggestion that Mr. Duggan was in London. The butler was a bald-faced liar, she thought, as she'd seen Duggan taking his usual morning ride along the edge of the property.

She would not give up that easily. She would make it her business to find out why Duggan coveted the Fairweather estate with a passion that seemed unnatural.

Miss Insatiable Curiosity, her mother had called her, but Cassie preferred to refer to herself as alert and inquisitive. Without really getting to the bottom of things, one could not find lasting solutions to problems, she reasoned.

The next day she waylaid him as he went out on his morning ride. It was easy, as he always took the same route.

He pulled in the reins as he spotted her on the path that bordered the Fairweather estate. "Mrs. Wenthaven," he greeted, his voice peevish. "I daresay you're standing in my way."

"I daresay I am," Cassie replied pointedly. "This way you can't avoid me, as you did yesterday."

"To my knowledge, I don't have any dealings with you."

"You're wrong there. As the steward of Fairweather, I must warn you that trespassing is a criminal offense. Your people have been seen overstepping their boundaries at every conceivable hour. This must stop, or I shall report you."

"Steward? That's the most ridiculous statement I've ever heard. Who ever met a female steward?" He laughed uproariously.

"You just did—for the first time, maybe, but it's true nevertheless. If you would kindly explain why you and your men are trespassing, perhaps we can all live in peace together."

He looked her up and down, no doubt taking in the shabby gray roundgown and pelisse she was wearing. If he threatened her, she wouldn't hesitate to use the stout walking stick she carried to emphasize her words.

"Mrs. Wenthaven, I'm not completely taken by surprise at your new profession. Wenthaven seems completely incapable of bestirring himself, other than to roll the dice at the gaming tables."

Cassie felt a wave of rage, which surprised her. She was never quick to anger, but this man had the contempt and the incivility to prompt her temper. "Don't underestimate Mr. Wenthaven," she said. "Now tell me, why are you so interested in Fairweather? I see no reason why we shouldn't be privy to your fascination. There's more than the acreage, isn't there?"

He twirled the reins around his hand. "I have no intention of informing you of my business, Mrs. Wenthaven. You cannot do anything to change the feud that has raged for a very long time between the Duggans and the Brookses."

"It does not sound like something worth upholding, especially since Mr. Wenthaven knows nothing about it."

"His interest never lay in family traditions. Over the years he must've visited here on all of five occasions. He's sitting on land that should belong to my family. It was *taken* from us brutally. I won't rest until the boundaries are restored."

Cassie tapped her walking stick on the ground.

"Let me remind you that the Fairweather estate has very little to offer, with its stony soil and its cliffs that present nothing but a sheer drop into the sea. The house is worth the going value of brick and mortar, and hardly even that."

"There are values you know nothing about, Mrs. Wenthaven, and I don't see any reason why I should have to explain myself. The Brookses were a ramshackle lot who, to my knowledge, never kept any records. But they wouldn't, seeing as most of their loot was taken illegally."

"I don't understand why this feud wasn't cleared up earlier. There has been plenty of time to think of suitable solutions. Decades and decades."

"Wenthaven's ancestors were in a much stronger position financially than the current one. There was never any opportunity to make a deal, and Seffington never had any interest in my offers, the cur! But things that were stolen shall be restored in my lifetime, mark my words."

"What things? Fairweather is an empty shell."

"Now it is, but was once rich, made rich on the backs of Duggans." He smacked the reins against the horse's neck. "Good day to you, Mrs. Wenthaven. I see no gain in keeping up this conversation."

"As long as you stop trespassing on the property, I have no quarrel with you," she called after him.

His reply was a harsh laugh and a glowering look over his shoulder.

Loot taken illegally, she thought as she quelled an angry retort and walked back over to Fairweather. What loot? Why had none of the Wenthavens mentioned it to her—or Seffington, for that matter? A feud would not just appear out of thin air. Her curiosity tickled, she decided to fight fire with fire. If

Duggan saw no crime in trespassing, he would be trespassed upon.

That night, as the moon hid behind a thick bank of clouds, she dressed in her plainest black mourning gown, tied a black hat over her hair, and donned a pair of black gloves. She slunk out the back door after the occupants of the house had fallen into blessed sleep. Picking up the walking stick she'd used earlier, she walked briskly across the park to Duggan's property. The air was still, somewhat spooky with the black masses of trees and bushes forming shapes that looked like hulking men ready to pounce on her.

She dismissed her misgivings and walked along the back of the Duggans' handsome mansion. Mr. Duggan had plenty of funds to keep up his estate. His doting sister and his daughter had gone to London for the girl's first Season. Cassie could hear laughter and the tinkling of glasses from the dining room. She slowed down, hiding behind some large shrubs. He had dinner guests, she thought. So much the better. That would keep Duggan out of his library.

Her heart thudded heavily as she swung herself up onto the terrace. Keeping away from any light coming through the windows, she hurried toward the double doors that led to the library. She knew its location; the windows faced the Fairweather estate. Once in a while during her walks, she'd seen Duggan framed in the window, his gaze fastened on Fairweather.

To her delight, the doors stood ajar. She slunk inside, her eyes getting used to the gloom. Soon she'd located a candle in a heavy candlestick on the desk and lighted it.

If only she had some kind of idea of what she was looking for. Her gaze darted over the desk littered with papers and accounts. She quickly riffled through them, finding nothing of interest. She tried the desk drawers, still finding nothing to catch her attention. After a thorough investigation of the bottom desk drawer, she got up and walked around the room, studying the portraits and the paintings. Well-fed Duggans stared down at her in hauteur.

In sharp contrast with the English portraits, she noticed some mounted old masks she could only label as ancient Egyptian. Replicas, no doubt. Duggan could not have real masks hanging on the walls. They would be priceless. Still, who would've thought he had such exotic tastes?

The tastes could've been brought down through generations. As far as she knew, the Duggans had been a seafaring family, just like the Brookses.

Lost in thought, she studied the artifacts on the walls and some smaller objects sitting under glass in display cabinets.

A few minutes later she heard footsteps in the hallway. As she rushed toward the terrace door, she crashed into a tall human shape concealed in a black cape. The man clamped a hard hand over her mouth and dragged her into a curtained alcove near the door.

"Shhhhh," he whispered fiercely as someone entered the room.

"I could've sworn I blew out all the candles," said Mr. Duggan, his voice tinged with annoyance. "A fire is the last thing I need in here."

Cassie stared into the dark eyes of her captor and listened to Duggan's footsteps crossing the floor. She pulled at the hand covering her mouth, and her captor, who she sensed was Dylan, loosened his grip.

They stood perfectly still, holding their breaths as Duggan strode across the room and blew out the candle. His steps retreated the way they'd come, and he closed the door with a slam. Cassie let out a long breath of relief.

"What are *you* doing here?" she hissed.

"I could ask the same of you," he whispered, so close she could feel his breath on her ear. "What would give you the harebrained idea of entering Duggan's house clandestinely?"

"Probably the same reason you're here. To find out more about that feud he's so eager to uphold," she murmured.

He let go of his convulsive grip on her shoulder and let his hand travel to the nape of her neck. That melting sensation came over her, and breathless anticipation rose in her chest. He leaned closer, as if loath to let go of her.

Forgetting their precarious situation, she completely opened up as his mouth came down hungrily on hers. The kiss deepened until she moaned with pleasure. Only a tiny part of her was screaming a warning in her head, and she had difficulty heeding it, even though she knew this was complete madness.

Gasping, she tore herself free. Her breath came ragged, and she had to lean against the wall to gather her composure.

He invaded her senses anew, but she put the flat of her hand against his chest. "No!" she hissed.

He backed away, pulling aside the curtain cautiously. He sounded breathless as he spoke. "Did you find anything of interest?"

"No, nothing. It would take a thorough search and keen observation of the surroundings to come up with some answers."

He made a sweep of the room on silent feet, stopping at the portraits and the artifacts, as she had done. As he came back, he whispered, "Did you find any papers in the desk?"

"Nothing that would explain the feud," she replied. "His accounts look very solid at first glance."

"Come, we'll have to look elsewhere," he said. He took her hand and led her out onto the terrace. "This is my problem, not yours. I never dreamed you would be this nosy."

"Inquisitive," she corrected him. "There's a world of difference."

"Whatever you say, my dear," he drawled and hauled her across the lawn to the shrubbery that bordered the estates. "Snooping through the neighbor's house is not one of your duties," he said as they reached Fairweather.

The moon came out from the clouds, and they stared at each other intently. Time seemed to stop once more.

"Whatever happened in there between us was naught but a spur of the moment excitement," he said, his voice unconvincing. "Inspired by the danger."

She shrugged her shoulders, still feeling as if she were floating among the stars. "Nothing happened," she said stonily. "Nothing whatsoever."

"From now on, concentrate on your duties around the estate, Cassie. Mr. Duggan isn't someone you can play with."

"He doesn't play by any kind of rules," she said, pulling off her gloves. Suddenly she felt suffocated in all the black.

"Cassie, I shall give you some orders first thing

tomorrow about the estate. Then I intend to leave for London."

She nodded, trying to ignore the unexpected feeling of emptiness his words created. "Good night, Dylan," she said and went into the house.

Merlin wound his sinewy body around Dylan's legs, and Dylan picked up the feline. "We'll never understand women, will we, Merlin?"

Who cares, Merlin seemed to respond as he butted his head against Dylan's jaw, purring. *Make the best of the present moment.*

Four

Dylan looked at Cassie's straight retreating figure and felt that tug on his heart again. He'd been so damned lonely since Dermott died. Life had tilted on its axis, and he would never be the same again.

Dermott had been his only true family. When all the other members failed at caring—including James, who'd cared only for himself—Dermott had filled the shoes of sibling, mother, and father. But more than that, as a twin he'd been completely aware of Dylan's thoughts and feelings. Connections like that were rare—especially within families. His only flaw had been excessive drinking.

Feeling the longing for his twin like lead in his stomach, he walked back to the house.

Even the next morning, Cassie felt shaken to the marrow. That Dylan's kisses had the power to do that frightened her no end. What had he been doing in Mr. Duggan's study? Well, looking for answers of course—just as she had. She would have to believe that, even if there might be more to the story.

Why was Mr. Duggan harboring such resent-

ment—to a point where he might put his threats into
action?

There had to be some account of the past somewhere. She recalled the dusty tomes she'd seen in
the attic and decided to go in search of them despite
the possibility of running across an army of mice.

Braced with a candlestick, she entered the attic.
The cobwebs seemed to have tripled since she last
set foot in this space. The musty aroma assaulted her
nose, and the shapes of trunks and old pieces of furniture did nothing to welcome her inside.

Setting her jaw, she marched forward, candlestick
in one hand. In the other she held a broom, with
which she cleared the cobwebs.

She found the trunk with the books and opened
the lid, fully expecting something unspeakable to leap
out at her, but nothing happened.

The attic felt closed in, the air unaccountably cold
and lifeless. She couldn't understand why the cold
seemed to intensify when she opened the trunk. It
was almost as if the atmosphere were clinging to her
skin with a life of its own. Creepy and clingy, it made
the hairs on her arms stand up.

With more hurry than she intended, she placed the
candlestick on the floor and dug through the contents
for the dusty tome she'd noticed before. She found
it and closed the trunk lid.

An urgency she did not recognize came over her.
She gathered up the book and the candlestick and
hurried from the room, slamming the door behind
her.

Trembling, she noticed the cold sensation had followed her onto the landing. Downstairs, as she entered the sunlit study, it disappeared. She could hear
Mrs. Granger's voice in her head. *That'll be Captain*

Brooks walking. Every noise at Fairweather the cook attributed to the dead pirate.

Cassie didn't believe in the superstitious drivel, but she'd heard the words repeated often enough.

Evidently Captain Brooks could walk through walls.

Dylan found Cassie sitting on a garden bench in the overgrown rose arbor near the vegetable garden, her head bent over a book. Her brown hair gleamed with red and golden highlights. He hadn't noticed before that the stray tendrils curled beguilingly on her neck.

The long white column of her neck looked vulnerable and so very feminine. He had a sudden urge to bend over her and plant a series of kisses along the slender arch.

She suddenly glanced up, the look in her brown eyes far away. He hadn't expected the smile that transformed her face. Her obvious delight surprised him, but it was soon clear his presence hadn't provoked her happiness.

She held up the worn volume. "I found this in the attic. It's an account of the the Brooks family and the building of Fairweather."

"At the time of the infamous Fortunatus Brooks?"

"Yes . . . and it's fascinating how they came to build this estate."

"It must've been beautiful at that time," he said, a tug of disappointment touching him as he gazed up at the dilapidated walls.

"Very. Fortunatus Brooks imported the best marble and the best stone to build this, a monument to his worldly success. Here's an account of the progress they made every day in building it. It took them three years to complete."

"He probably designed it himself, seeing as the decorations still intact are in the more extravagant taste of the 1600s." He glanced at the crumbling stone gargoyles at the corner of the roof, then at the marble terrace. " 'Tis unfortunate the marble has gone to ruin."

"He was a sea captain and would've seen many wondrous things to inspire his architecture," she said.

He gazed at her, at the soft hair he'd touched as he kissed her and the full curves of her mouth that now inspired him to kiss her again. But he didn't move.

"Foreign motifs certainly inspired him," she continued. "According to this book, he studied design everywhere he traveled. He was fascinated with architecture."

He shook himself out of his daze. "I don't doubt that for a moment. He pirated all kinds of patterns, I'm sure."

"Do I detect a hint of sarcasm?" She tilted her head like a bird and smiled at him.

Why was it that James's widow had such a dauntingly beautiful smile when she usually looked so prim and proper? He couldn't answer that, but his gut told him he should stay away from her or forever be entranced. The word *entranced* startled him. She had no power over him—none at all.

"They built this place with some efforts at security. Evidently some of the rooms have double walls and there are secret chambers. Not that I've come across any as I explored," she said, "but old buildings like this often do. They had a place to hide treasure in case of an attack. The seventeenth century was a violent time."

"People were very uncivilized in those days, weren't they?" he said.

He raised his foot onto the bench were she was sitting and leaned his elbow on his knee, noticing the beguiling curl of her eyelashes as she lowered her gaze. A faint blush rose in her cheeks. She looked for a long moment at his leg, so close to her, and a delicate pulse beat at her temple.

"Uncivilized? No more than they are today." She gave his leg a pointed look.

He enjoyed provoking her and leaned even closer.

"I found a few handwritten pages in the back of the book," she continued, stiffening as his boot rubbed against her thigh. She moved aside a few inches. "They are so old that they are crumbling, but not as old as the tome itself. Weatherworn, I suspect."

"What do they say?" He moved his foot an inch closer, but she didn't shy away.

"The account was written a hundred years ago. It tells about the ghost of Captain Brooks and how he hasn't been able to find peace."

She wrinkled her brow and chewed on her lower lip as if debating with herself.

"Is that all?"

"Yes." She hesitated. "Yes, there's really nothing that would interest you, especially since you'll be going back to London any day now."

"Are you telling me to go back to London?" He smiled at her, noticing her nervousness.

"No, not at all, but the tedium of the countryside must be irking you by now."

"There's no reason to tell me what I'm feeling,"

he drawled. "Perhaps I enjoy a sojourn in the country."

"I doubt it," she said crisply. "One doesn't change one's habits overnight. I'm sure you're used to the glitter and excitement of the metropolis."

"That I am, but there's nothing wrong with variety."

"I would think you would grow restless in a bucolic idyll like this."

"If I grow restless, there's nothing like a brisk horse ride to take the edge off. That's the same whether I'm here or in the metropolis." He nudged the toe of his boot closer to her and saw her shoulders stiffen. "It really sounds as if you're eager to get rid of me."

"As long as you linger here, I can't very well step into my new position as steward."

He chuckled and noticed the small frown between her eyes. "You don't like it that I have taken over the command. When you lived here with only the Elderberry twins and the servants for company, you held the reins of the household."

"I don't see a lot of change taking place," she retorted, ice in her voice. "The roof is still leaking."

"I'm taking inventory of the things that need to be accomplished." He read the feelings crossing her face, knowing she was thinking he hadn't done anything to move things forward. And he hadn't. He felt uncomfortable for a fleeting moment, but truth to tell, he didn't have to report to her, did he?

He paused. "I can see your desire to tell me exactly what needs to be done." She opened her mouth to speak, but he held up his hand. "Yes, I know you've been living here for a lot longer than I have."

"It's highly overbearing of you to put words into my mouth."

"You haven't said anything," he said and put his fingertip under her chin. He looked into her eyes, which were blazing by now. He continued, "Just the idea that I would actually *do* anything to improve matters around here is an immense notion. Overwhelming, in fact. *Everything* needs to be replaced."

Some of her anger died down. She moved her head away from his touch. "I can see that dilemma, but an estate that has been in the family for that long is worth restoring."

He studied the crumbling facade. "The only thing thriving around here is the ivy taking over the walls," he commented glumly.

"I'd say some of the structure is still solid. At least stone doesn't rot."

"If it did, nothing would be left." His mood to tease her had gone and he lowered his boot to the ground.

"There are drawings about every area of the house in this book. You could use them as a guideline for the restoration."

Something akin to a burden settled on his shoulders. Her unspoken challenge was clear to him. She expected him to rebuild the estate, and maybe he had to if he wanted to salvage his name—and his pride. He knew if she had the funds and the permission, nothing could stop her from moving forward on the project. She was even now looking with keen interest at the ramshackle structure as if it were *her* mission, not his.

"It's a pity there are no female architects," she said, more to herself than to him, but he could discern the chagrin in her voice.

"You sound as if you would've liked a man's education."

She looked at him as if searching for more sarcasm, but he was sincere. "I would've enjoyed the opportunity of expanding my knowledge. Embroidery and watercolors don't present my mind with any kind of challenge."

"How about arranging tea parties?" He smiled as he saw the mutiny in her eyes. "Don't bludgeon me with that book."

"Life is tedious if it is reduced to the trivial choices of whether to serve crumpets or currant cake."

"My mother made quite and art out of it, if I remember correctly," he said, recalling her rather simple tastes and her delight in the smallest things. The woman in front of him presented more of a fighting spirit, maybe even that of a general. "It's perhaps a pity you weren't born a man, Cassie. You would have made a splendid addition to Wellington's staff in the Peninsula."

"I'm not interested in warfare, only strategy."

"Quite," he replied, wondering how his lame-witted brother James had dealt with this formidable woman. He probably hadn't dealt at all, just left her to her own devices. A pity, really. He doubted anyone really knew Cassie Wenthaven, but he was sure he would if he stuck around Fairweather long enough. How long that would be was anyone's guess. It depended on how long boredom would take to settle in. It always did.

The thought made him uncomfortable. He nodded at Cassie. "I'm curious to see what Mrs. Granger has produced for the dinner table. She always performs culinary miracles."

Without another word, he returned to the house.

The door creaked ominously as he closed it behind him.

Cassie watched his broad back as he left, warring feelings running through her. One part of her was hopelessly attracted to him as she remembered their kisses. The other side didn't want anything to do with him. She didn't trust what he represented—the spoiled, idle aristocrat who thought more of his nights on the town than of doing something worthwhile. She had seen the value in purpose as she'd watched her father tend to his flock, her mother right beside him.

She gazed at the drooping roofline of the mansion and heaved a deep sigh. If she owned the pile, she would do anything to bring it back to its former glory. She could see the potential, and she knew what had to be done.

If only she had some say in the matter. But she might as well surrender her desire to work on the house. With Dylan at the helm, it was unlikely anything would come of the restoration. The thought made her unbelievably sad.

She heard the baby cry in the kitchen and she rounded the overgrown vegetation to enter through the back. The baby appeared inconsolable as Mrs. Granger swung him on one arm and tried to stir a pot with the other. A mouthwatering aroma of stew and vegetables reached Cassie's nose.

She rescued the baby from the harried cook.

"Does naught but pine after his mum, he does," Mrs. Granger grumbled. "If I could just lay me hands on that heartless woman, I would tell her a few truths."

"Sooner or later we'll find her."

"The constable came 'round here to ask me all kinds of questions." She huffed and put down the wooden ladle with a decisive bang. "He sounded as if he wanted to accuse me of bein' the mother."

Cassie cradled the crying baby in her arms and crooned softly. "I take it he didn't have any knowledge of who the mother is?"

"No one has had a baby in these parts in the last sixmonth, and he hadn't heard any rumors of a child missing. The mother sneaked up here in the dark from nowhere and put the basket with the infant on our doorstep." She wagged her head from side to side. "As if we need the added burden of lookin' after it."

The boy quieted down, and Cassie placed the milk-soaked corner of a napkin in his mouth. He sucked heartily, waving his tiny hands. His tear-soaked face tugged at her heartstrings. The little lad had done nothing to find himself abandoned on the doorstep of some stranger's house.

"He's tearin' down the roof with his caterwaulin', he is," Mrs. Granger complained as she cut up a loaf of bread and placed the pieces in a basket. "I'll be deaf for life if things don't change around here."

"Surely you're exaggerating, Mrs. Granger," Cassie said, thinking the baby wrinkled his forehead in the exact fashion of Dylan Wenthaven. Then there was the silver rattle.

The thought that Dylan might be the father and not care one iota about it bothered her more than she could imagine. He'd taken one cursory glance in the basket and dismissed the babe. She had no doubt the man was a wastrel and a womanizer.

The child started crying again, and Cassie felt

guilty for thinking such negative thoughts of the might-be father.

"There, there, you shall soon rest in the comforts of your mother's arms," she crooned and swung the baby gently until he quieted down with a series of hiccups.

Acting as a guardian, Merlin the cat lay on the floor at the end of the basket as she put the boy inside.

Just as the infant started drifting off to sleep, she heard a commotion at the front door. She discerned the animated voices of the Elderberry twins and Ned Biggins's gravelly one. Someone had entered with what sounded like mountains of luggage as the thuds of trunks against floorboards filled the hallway.

Bringing the baby, she went to see what the disturbance was all about. The Elderberry twins fluttered like moths around a tall, handsome young man dressed in the latest fashion of a drab riding coat with twelve capes, buckskins, a coat of blue superfine, polished top boots that rivaled the shine of his giant smile, and a cravat whose elegant folds would've taken hours in front of the mirror to arrange.

Piled on the floor around him stood trunks, one of which Ned was trying to haul over the threshold of the open front door.

"Of all the angels in heaven," Hazel Elderberry twittered. Hermione echoed her words.

Angels? Cassie thought to herself.

Dylan stormed out of the study. At first she thought he was angry, but then she noticed the joy on his face.

"Edward Bunney!" he shouted. "I didn't think you

would make the effort to visit me here in this bucolic spot, even though you swore you would."

"Old boy, I never go back on my word," Edward said as he pulled his gloves off, one tight finger after the other. He flicked an imaginary speck of dust from his sleeve. "Deuced dusty on the roads."

"Did you drive your curricle?"

Edward nodded. "Yes, and I have a pair of new nags to pull it, perfectly matched bays. Sweet goers. You have to try them as soon as the opportunity presents itself."

"I don't suppose I should ask you how you acquired such fine horseflesh."

Bunney's eyebrows rose a notch and he looked down his nose. "You shouldn't."

He had a very fine pair of brown eyes, Cassie noted, but something about him rubbed her the wrong way. Maybe it was the way he was striking a pose or the way he was pulling at those dratted gloves. And when he discarded his hat on top of one of the trunks, she took umbrage at the artificial Byronic fall of his curls.

The Elderberry twins fluttered their fans and made unintelligible noises. They had probably never met such a grandiose personage.

"How remiss of me," Dylan said as if suddenly remembering their presence. His quick glance at Cassie held a hint of an apology. "This is James's widow, Mrs. Wenthaven," he said. "Cassie, meet my best friend, Mr. Edward Bunney."

Cassie nodded coolly. "A great pleasure, I'm sure," she said, her voice at its most crisp. Mr. Bunney made an elegant bow. It must have taken a few years to perfect, she thought uncharitably, but immediately chastised herself for being judgmental.

Dylan went on to introduce the elderly lodgers.

"We can make good use of the young man," Hazel said as she eyed Mr. Bunney with appreciation. She blushed as Hermione nudged her with her bony elbow. "What I mean is we need someone to help us sort through our skeins of silk. He seems nimble-fingered enough."

"I don't doubt he is," Cassie said, "but I daresay he takes little interest in embroidery silks."

"Piffle! The young man wouldn't be so rude as to turn down an opportunity to help us crippled old ladies," Hazel said, and Hermione echoed her words. "We can be most persuasive."

"Is that a good haunch of venison I smell?" Mr. Bunney asked, turning his nose in the direction of the kitchen. "I admit I'm famished."

Dylan threw Cassie a penetrating glance, and she shot an ice-cold one back.

"I'm sure there's enough stew for one more. If we'd had some advance notice, we would have found something more interesting to serve at the dinner table," she said. "As it is, stew and bread and mashed turnips will be served shortly. And I must confess we haven't polished the silver." *As if we ever had any.*

"Never mind," Mr. Bunney said with his radiant smile. "There's no food I dislike, and if I have to eat with my fingers, I shall find a way."

You're a terrible liar to boot, she thought. He had never eaten anything with his fingers, except bonbons or other sweetmeats. "We don't have to stoop to that," she said. "I'm sure you'll find the cutlery quite adequate."

"I'm sorry," he said with another grin. "I didn't mean to imply your table lacked in any way."

There has to be some Irish blood in his veins some-where, Cassie thought. That slippery tongue belonged on the Emerald Isle, surely. "It never occurred to me," Cassie said.

The Elderberry twins cried out in horror as the young man discarded the many-caped coat with Ned's help. It became obvious he was wearing one arm in a black silk sling, probably the reason he'd worked off the gloves so slowly. He didn't show a face of great pain, though, Cassie thought.

"Good God, what happened to you?" Dylan exclaimed.

"Got run through in a duel. Not a bad cut, just a scratch, really, but it was deu—terribly painful at the time."

The twins twittered. "You poor, poor man. No wonder you wanted to recuperate in the country. The air around here is excessively invigorating," Hazel said. "I can't sleep a wink at night because of it."

Cassie gave the old lady a searching look. She could've sworn she heard rhythmic snoring coming from the twins' room every evening. They always retired early, as they were very early risers.

Hazel and Hermione each gently gripped one of Mr. Bunney's elbows and led him toward the dilapidated dining room at the end of the hallway. Cassie hung back, still cradling the infant, who was now fast asleep. She pinned Dylan with a hard stare.

"You said nothing to me about visitors, let alone overnight guests. Who is going to carry those trunks upstairs, and where are we going to put him?"

"I never thought Eddie would take me up on the invitation," Dylan said sheepishly. "He detests the countryside. It's most peculiar."

"I take it you have no idea how long he plans to stay here."

Dylan shook his head. "As far as I'm concerned, he's welcome for as long as he likes. My house is his house. We've always shared everything. Well, almost everything. He was great comfort when Dermott died."

Yes, Dermott, Cassie thought. The wilder twin, James had always called him. Cassie had a vague memory of Dermott lying drunk across a table at her wedding. All she'd seen of him was the back of his head as his neckcloth rested in a puddle of sauce. She abhorred excess drinking. She had seen it ruin too many lives in her father's parish.

"I don't know how we'll feed him in style," Cassie grumbled as she headed toward the kitchen to put the baby back into the basket so that Mrs. Granger could keep an eye on him while they were eating.

"Hunting never went out of style," Dylan said. "As Ned will confirm."

"Yes, I'm sure rabbit stew will abound," Cassie said as a parting shot before entering the kitchen door.

She joined the company in the dining room shortly and found that Mrs. Granger had found a much-repaired tablecloth somewhere and thrown it on the table before putting the stew out. She'd even found a vase for a ragged bunch of wildflowers, which she must have picked in a hurry in the overgrown back garden. Bluebells clung to daisies and buttercups, and even a few stalwart straws of timothy had found their way into the bouquet.

Dylan fetched a decanter of sherry from the sideboard and poured the liquid into glasses, which he distributed with the flair of a butler. He'd missed his calling, Cassie thought as he handed her the glass. Whatever that calling was.

He gave her a knowing glance, his eyes narrowing as if he could read her irreverent thought. She couldn't understand why she felt so much on edge and so uncivilized. It was as if every one of her thoughts had barbs attached to them. Ever since Dylan had returned to his ancestral home, her world had been turned upside down.

Not only had she been forced to face the fact that she lived completely at his mercy, but all peace had been taken away from her when he kissed her that first time. The nerve of the man. The reaction had been delayed, but now it was hitting her with full force. And for some strange reason, she felt as if she was responsible for the tattered tablecloth and the peeling walls. Maybe she could have done something to repair things during the time she'd stayed at Fairweather, but with what funds?

She had lived here on Lord Seffington's mercy, and he hadn't seen fit to rescue the failing estate, so why should she feel in any way guilty?

She pasted a smile on her face as everyone toasted. The sherry disappeared in the blink of an eye, and the Elderberry twins giggled.

"We usually don't hold with drinking anything but lemonade, but a glass of sherry now and again can be so *comforting,* don't you agree, Hermione?" Hazel said.

Hermione fluttered her pale eyelashes and sucked in her lips as if tasting the last of the sweet wine. "So very *comforting* indeed," she nearly whispered.

With that observation, everyone sat down to the simple meal.

Dylan asked Mr. Bunney, "So tell me about this

latest adventure that put your arm in a sling, Eddie. It must've happened recently, as it's only about two weeks since I last saw you."

Mr. Bunney moaned. "I hope your sensibilities are strong enough to hear my tale of woe," he said to the ladies.

"We're made with a core of steel even if we look frail," Hazel said, "and nothing can ruffle Cassie's feathers. A more levelheaded lady is hard to find."

"Thank you," Cassie said, not feeling levelheaded in the slightest, but rather giddy.

Mr. Bunney leaned back in his chair for effect and patted the arm that rested in the sling. "I've been smote with Cupid's arrow," he said dolefully. His voice trembled as he said the word "Cupid," and Cassie braced herself for some melodramatic tale.

"I met this beautiful creature with hair of spun gold and the largest blue eyes I've ever encountered at Lady Gassington's ball. This young lady is innocence personified, and so full of grace and beauty that my heart aches just from thinking about her."

"Really," Cassie said at her most driest.

"Really," Mr. Bunney repeated and gave her a soulful look.

"Don't interrupt, dear Cassie," Hazel admonished. "I know I'll cry at the end of this tale." She fished around in the pocket of her faded gown for a handkerchief, and a big tear was already rolling down her cheek.

"So I am stunned by an arrow straight into my heart. I could hardly breathe as I noted every detail of her delightful being, from the tips of her golden eyelashes to the tips of her tiny slippers. She's a fairy princess, whom I think about every waking moment of my day. No one ever told me how *painful* love can be," he said as if surprised by his own words. "Every waking moment is an agony of longing." He gave everyone a dramatic glance. "I think I'm wasting away. Today is the first day in a week I've felt like eating anything."

Cassie could not recall feeling anything remotely like that for James. In fact, she hadn't felt any kind of longing for him.

"I'd die for one more glance from her angelic eyes," Mr. Bunney said, his lower lip starting to tremble slightly. "I'm in the throes of the worst fever, and there seems to be no end in sight."

"It does sound like some kind of strange disease." Dylan gave Cassie an enigmatic glance. Her stomach tightened oddly, and she looked away quickly.

"I could go into very much detail of the agonies I have suffered, but I don't want to upset your tender sensibilities, ladies."

"We're already suffering with you," Hazel said, dabbing at her reddening eyes. "I've never heard anything so romantic."

"I found a way to be introduced to this Vision of Delight, and I discovered this is her first Season in London. She's only seventeen years old, but wise beyond her years."

"You're a cradle robber, Eddie," Dylan said.

"I did say she's wise beyond her years," Mr. Bunney said loftily. "I danced twice with her, and when we first took to the floor, she gave me this most beautiful smile. As long as I live, I shall never forget it. I declare 'twill be the last thing on my mind on my deathbed."

Definitely Irish blood running in his veins, Cassie thought, tapping her toe on the floor with impatience.

"I held her soft hand in mine, and I will never

be the same again," he continued mournfully. "I did not eat or sleep for the next three days, only thought of her."

"So how did you come by that wound?" Dylan prodded.

"I tried to find ways to see her. I never was invited to tea, nor did I receive any kind of encouragement from her dragon of a chaperone. They would receive visitors between eleven and half past eleven, but I had to watch a gaggle of ogling suitors make fools of themselves over this Vision."

"What is her name?" Hazel asked.

"Giselle, and she comes from a very wealthy family. From what I know, the father is an ogre and a country bumpkin with a hot temper, and her aunt is a stickler for propriety. She's Lady Cutting."

"Octogenarian if she's a day," Hazel said. "I remember in my time when she—"

"She's older than Methuselah," Mr. Bunney said hotly, and earned a withering glance from his elderly table companion. "Anyway, her father rarely goes up to London, but he was there the fateful day when Lady Cutting and my fair Giselle were taking the air in Green Park. It turns out that the lady of my heart has a very soft heart for all winged creatures," he said with a sigh.

"Do you mean bats and flies?" Cassie couldn't help but asking. The sherry must've gone to her head.

Mr. Bunney gave her a startled glance. "Not at all! I'm talking about birds. She had brought some bread for the swans at the Serpentine, and I happened to be riding by as a lackey was handing her down. I jumped out of the saddle and spread my cloak on the grass for Giselle to step on, and she smiled at me most prettily. I must say I trembled so much that

I could barely remain standing upright. And when Giselle tripped, I rushed forward to catch her. I think the heel of her slipper caught in the folds of my cloak." His voice turned gravelly with emotion. "For one endless moment, I held her in my arms."

"Then what happened?" Dylan asked.

"She was wrenched from me in the most unceremonious fashion, and the dragon was screaming in the carriage. Then this gentleman full of vengeance bore down on me and slapped my face with his glove. It was most embarrassing." Mr. Bunney grimaced. "It turned out to be Giselle's father, and he told me to have my seconds meet his to set up a confrontation at Barn Elms." His sigh filled the room. "Needless to say, I was furious. Not only had I caught Giselle and prevented her from sustaining grievous injury, but I had protected her delicate slippers from the mud."

"I'd say it was a most chivalrous gesture," Dylan said, laughter in his voice.

"I met the madman at Barn Elms two days later at dawn, and he turned out to be a fiend with a sword. I admit I was out of practice. He ran me through the arm, and that would've been the end of it, except for the fact that I will surely die if I can't see my fair Giselle again." His voice turned even more mournful. "I might still die if the wound becomes poisonous. My valet, who by the way is sleeping in the curricle, said the wind blowing in his face on the way here took its toll on him—"

"Sleeping in the curricle?" Dylan asked. "There's no room to really stretch out."

"He's used to sleeping sitting up. Something strange with his breathing apparatus. The man is a godsend, so I can't hold some small oddities against him." Mr. Bunney bit into the last piece of bread and chewed as if it were the last thing he would ever eat.

"Giselle . . . hmm, it sounds faintly familiar, but I can't quite place her," Dylan mused aloud.

"Mr. Duggan has a daughter named Giselle," Cassie said.

Mr. Bunney brightened. "That's it! Giselle Duggan, heiress to Lady Cutting's massive fortune."

Dylan shook his head. "So now we know why you're really here."

"Some other aunt of Miss Duggan turned up her toes, so Giselle had to break off her Season to go into mourning. It's a most dashed business." He slapped his hand to his mouth. "I apologize."

"Young man," Hazel said stalwartly, "you've come to the right place. We shall help you to salvage True Love. After all, we have years more experience than you have, Mr. Bunney, and we know all about love, don't we, Hermione?"

Hermione nodded. "Yes . . ." she said hesitantly.

As far as Cassie could recall, the twins had never been married or even engaged.

She sighed. This would be the end of peace and quiet as she knew it.

Five

"You poor, poor young man," Hazel exclaimed. She put her thin hand to her heart. "I can't remember when I've been that moved, and to think you have to deal with Mr. Duggan is too much to bear. He wouldn't know true love if it knocked him over the head."

"Hazel is right, old friend," Dylan said. "Mr. Duggan will be a great obstacle to true love. And if he already took a dislike to you, 'tis likely he'll never change, no matter whether you're in the right or in the wrong."

Mr. Bunney looked morose and cradled his injured arm. "I've suffered enough. Look at me; what a pitiful sight. But you have to give me some credit for trying to save the lady of my heart from breaking her ankle."

"Perhaps if you approach Mr. Duggan like a sensible suitor—ask him for his permission to court Giselle," Cassie suggested.

"Don't think I haven't pondered that avenue, but I have to confess he wouldn't look favorably at my suit." Mr. Bunney looked pained. "I'm not a great catch, you see. He would judge me as a fortune hunter, which is far from the truth. Any one of my friends could tell you I would marry only for love. A fortune means nothing to me."

Fiddlesticks, Cassie thought. She gave Dylan a questioning glance and he looked uncomfortable for a moment, but rallied.

"Of course you're right, Eddie. You're a romantic at heart, and I know your intentions are honorable."

"Perhaps Mr. Duggan would appreciate any show of gainful employment that might prove you're capable of taking care of Miss Giselle," Cassie said dampeningly.

Mr. Bunney looked at her in horror. "Employment? I'll have you know right now I'll never stoop that low. It's inconceivable I could support Giselle in the style she's accustomed to unless I win a fortune at the gaming tables or at Newmarket."

Cassie froze as the truth dawned on her that another gambler had landed or her doorstep. "The odds of winning are slim," she said icily, "and if you win, you won't be able to stop yourself from gambling it all away."

Mr. Bunney shrugged his shoulders. "Well, that's part of the charm of gambling, isn't it? The thrill, the uncertainty, the heart-stopping excitement."

"And the ruin to everyone around you," Cassie said sharply. " 'Tis the height of irresponsibility."

Everyone grew quiet, and Mr. Bunney's face took on a deeply injured look.

Cassie moved uncomfortably in her chair. "What I'm implying is that anyone with enough mental agility to learn the strategy of card games has the ability to learn useful business skills, which in turn will lend opportunity and stability to one's life."

"Just imagine how utterly boring that would be,"

Mr. Bunney exclaimed. "I would wither away with ennui."

Hazel and Hermione exchanged uncertain glances. Their dashing romantic knight might be showing some tarnish on his armor. Cassie watched him squirm, and she slanted a glance in Dylan's direction. He had leaned back in his chair and crossed his arms over his chest. A glitter of something burned in the depths of his eyes, but she couldn't read his expression, and the rest of his face gave no hint of his emotions.

"That business would be preferable to gambling is a narrow opinion, but one you're entitled to, Cassie," he said, no hint of harshness in his words.

"Well, thank you." She felt deflated. "It depends from which side of the fence you're looking, from the side of common sense or that of castles in the air."

"You would always look from the side of common sense, wouldn't you?" Dylan said, the corners of his mouth lifting.

"There's nothing wrong with that," Hazel cried in Cassie's defense. "If it weren't for Cassie, we would be in the poorhouse, and this house would be filled with filth and rats, mark my words. Everything might be threadbare around here, but it's clean and orderly. And she's not beyond using a hammer and nails, either. She's patched many a leak, but I believe the house is getting the better of us, so it's about time you take over the responsibility for this heap."

Dylan bowed his head in acknowledgment. "I've heard nothing but since I returned, and I do see the need."

"Something concrete as in restoring this house might give you the same sense of adventure as gambling might," Hazel said, and Cassie was surprised to hear such a shrewd observation from the lady who had confessed many times to having a simple mind.

"Probably more so," Dylan said wryly, "but also a lot more headache."

"And commitment," Cassie added. "Quite a challenge."

Dylan drawled, his eyes narrowed, "Aren't we getting off the subject of how to help Eddie attain his true love?"

"The way things are, I doubt Mr. Duggan will turn a favorable eye on Mr. Bunney's proposal to court Miss Giselle."

"That's why we have to come up with a workable plan!" Mr. Bunney cried. "I have to save her life or something—or his, so that he's eternally indebted to me."

"And how do you propose to do that?" Cassie asked. "You can't stage an accident just so you can save someone's life."

Mr. Bunney shrugged. "Why not? No one will be hurt."

"How are you so sure about that?" Cassie asked sharply. "You'll have to make it look real."

"But it'll be staged. There's a world of difference."

"I can't hold with your plan to go about your courtship with manipulation and possibly put someone's life in jeopardy. That's completely outside moral behavior."

"All's fair in love and war," Mr. Bunney said, two red spots burning in his cheeks.

"Only for those for whom it's convenient," Cassie said, feeling prickly. This conversation was bringing up deeper issues than what it had promised when Mr. Bunney launched into his romantic woes. She wasn't sure she'd be able to stay under the same roof as Mr. Bunney after his casual disclosure of possible ways to gain Miss Giselle's hand.

"If you truly love someone, you wouldn't want to do something underhanded to gain their approval," she said. "It's wholly irresponsible to think such love would last past the first blush."

"What is love to you, then?" Dylan challenged, and Cassie had no clue how they had entered such deep waters just over a bowl of stew and in front of a stranger.

Seeing the confronting glint in his eyes, she had to reply or slink away in shame. "Love is maturity, to be able to see and accept all the flaws and still hold that other person dear in your heart. Love is commitment and trust. Love is willingness to listen, to give even when you don't feel like giving because you place that person's well-being in front of your own. Love is support and a willingness to be supported in your own weakness."

"I doubt you would ever be weak, Cassie."

"You don't know me very well, and I doubt you ever will take the time to really know someone," she said, feeling a wave of disappointment as she uttered the words.

"What you said about love, Cassie, is very beautiful," Hazel commented and dabbed at her eyes. "You spoke with such *longing*."

"Yes," echoed Hermione. "Such longing."

Cassie blushed, unable to stand another moment of being the center of attention. She put down her napkin and rose from her chair. "I think I'll find out if Mrs. Granger has made some apple tarts. She was talking about it this morning."

The gentlemen rose immediately in a gesture of politeness.

Before anyone could comment on her red cheeks, Cassie fled from the room. She closed the door behind her and leaned momentarily against the wall. She put her hand against her racing heart and wondered if she'd ever be able to look into Dylan's eyes again after all she'd said. He would surely believe she was an utter fool, but why should she care? To her chagrin, she found she cared a lot about his opinion. Why, she didn't know. She hardly knew the man, even if he was her brother-in-law.

She headed toward the kitchen, but stopped in her tracks as she heard a commotion by the front door. *Another* arrival in one day?

She hurried to the foyer and found a slight and dazed gentleman looking around as if lost. She immediately suspected this was Mr. Bunney's valet, who evidently slept sitting upright. He did somewhat appear as if he had an iron poker in his back. He hooked her with a dark eye and said in disbelief, "I daresay Mr. Bunney is really in the suds now."

"You must be Mr.—"

"Mr. Ripple at your service, madam." He made a bow, not too deep, not too shallow. "Can you hint me in the direction of my master's suite?"

"I'm afraid we don't offer suites here, and we haven't decided where to put Mr. Bunney yet."

"Oh . . . my." The valet clapped his mouth shut and gazed at her with disapproval. His nose was hooked and his skin sallow, his dark hair pomaded and curled in the latest fashion. *There must be Mediterranean blood in his veins somewhere,* she thought. "We live a simple life here. I'm Mrs. Wenthaven, and together we'll find an accommodation for your master and you."

She led the way up the stairs, and he followed, his step small and rapid.

"Ohh, did you feel the cold air on the landing, Mrs. Wenthaven?" His voice took on a hint of apprehension. "I know I'm taking a great liberty as I speak up, but I believe you have a ghost on the premises. I've always been sensitive to such occurrences."

"You're not the first one to speak of that, but I personally don't believe in ghosts." He'd been right about the waft of chilly air that had met them on the landing, but then the house had many drafts. " 'Tis said the man who built this estate, Captain Brooks, walks these halls."

"I'm certain of it," the little man said. "Not an unpleasant man in his day, but quite forceful."

"He's said to have been a pirate."

"Something says he's not been able to find peace in the afterlife. Mayhap the memories of his crimes on the seas keep him from eternal rest."

"I doubt it," Cassie said, thinking that Captain Brooks probably didn't have much of a conscience. She led the way down the musty upstairs hallway and picked the bedchamber she knew had no leaks and the fewest drafts. She opened the door and found that Mrs. Granger had had the same idea of where to put Mr. Bunney and had opened all the windows. She was in the process of putting sheets on the bed.

At least the room was swept once a week, so it didn't lack in cleanliness, but the bleakness of the peeling paint and scanty rugs could not be hidden with the sweep of the broom or a swab with the mop. She could literally see Mr. Ripple wrinkle his nose, but at least he had the good manners to make no comment.

"I shall immediately set up Mr. Bunney's things," the valet said and moved efficiently across the room.

Cassie introduced Mrs. Granger to the dapper little man, and the cook greeted him with a shrewd look. Cassie hoped they would get along. She feared there would be plenty of tension in the house once Mr. Duggan got wind of Mr. Bunney's presence at Fairweather.

Feeling her own tension rising at the thought, she left the room. In the last few hours everything had turned topsy-turvy; in the last week her whole life had changed. It wasn't strange that she felt a little apprehensive.

She returned to the kitchen to find Ned Biggins peering into the baby basket.

"The wee tyke is sleepin' peacefully. I can't remember when I ever slept that calmly—without a care in the world."

"Yes, the burden seems to get heavier with the years, doesn't it, Ned?"

"Aye."

"Did Mrs. Granger make any apple tarts?"

"That would be the day," Ned said and scratched his head. "The apples from last year are all finished."

Cassie sighed and glanced around the bare table. "I'll have to inform the others that dinner is over." She lifted the ancient account of the building of Fairweather from the chair where she'd left it.

Clutching the old tome in her arms, she wondered if Captain Brooks was watching her even now. The thought gave her chills. She bent over the basket, debating whether to bring the baby with her.

"I'll look after the boy until Mrs. Granger comes

back downstairs," Ned said. "Then I'll start bringing the trunks upstairs."

Cassie went back to the dining room and found that the others had already left. She could hear the Elderberry twins on their way to their room, and men's voices came from the study. Dylan was probably getting an account of the latest gossip from the metropolis.

Thoughtful, she returned to the dining room and set the old tome on an empty chair. She stacked the dishes for later removal. Mrs. Granger surely was a gem, as she made an effort every day to put nourishing meals on the table. Cassie piled the empty bread basket and the cutlery to one side and gathered the napkins.

The old account had hinted at double walls, but never explained where they were in the house. If the writer had described the location, enemies would've found any hidden treasures within.

She glanced at the peeling paint and stepped up to a section of the wall that had nothing but two rusty nails hammered into it. Perhaps something would appear if she looked closely enough—a line, a crack that hid a secret door. It couldn't be that easy. Someone would've found it if it were in plain view. Nevertheless, she slid her hand over the cool surface, finding nothing but unyielding wall.

She searched intently for twenty minutes. If there was a secret door, she couldn't find any visible clues. Shrugging her shoulders, she addressed the air. "Captain Brooks, if you're really hovering, you'll have to give me a helping hand, but I admit I'd be surprised if there's a treasure."

She listened to the silence, but didn't notice any changes in the atmosphere. She didn't hear any voices or ghostly footsteps. It would take a lot to convince her the ghost existed. Mrs. Granger's belief had made no impact on her, but how did Mr. Ripple know about the supposed specter? He had no previous knowledge of it—or did he?

" 'Tis all balderdash," she said to herself. "Ghosts are something fevered writers' imaginations have concocted over the centuries." The observation sounded somewhat hollow, but she pinched her lips together.

Bringing the tome to the table, she carefully opened it. The musty smell rose pungent from the pages, and black blobs of mold obscured some of the text. Captain Brooks's spidery handwriting covered every space of the page except for the careful diagrams he'd drawn all through the account.

She deciphered some of the antiquated English. It was slow going, but she had helped her father in the past to interpret church records.

"I have now a magnificent home in which to display my treasures, things so valuable and so splendid that their equal can't be found anywhere."

She added her own opinion. "Well, if you had such treasures, they are long gone, Captain Brooks. And if you had them, they were not gainfully earned. You stole them from somewhere, mayhap from someone who suffered from the loss. But you didn't think of the consequences."

She glanced out the window as if seeking comfort from the sunlight outside. The blood of a ruthless plunderer ran in Dylan's veins. No wonder he was drawn to gambling; the wildness ran deep at the core of his being. She could easily picture him two hundred years ago on a pirate ship with a cutlass in his hand and a black patch over his eye. He would've had that wicked grin that he had now, she mused, frowning.

Captain Brooks probably had had that same smile—if he had ever smiled.

Something obscured the sunlight outside and a sudden rumble came from above. A rain cloud had moved in from the sea and what had been a sunny day had turned into a sullen gray haze. The wind whipped through the window, billowing out the tattered lace curtains.

A chill came over her just as the rain started pelting down. Shivers ran down her spine, and she hurried to close the windows. How could the weather have changed so quickly, and where was the cold coming from?

She drew the curtains across the panes, but the chill persisted. If she didn't know better, she could've sworn the fog had moved into the room. Preposterous! She blinked hard, and when she opened her eyes, the fog was gone.

The wind had raised some of the pages of the old book, and they were gently fluttering down to lie still. She took a deep, trembling breath and her heartbeat settled into a slower rhythm.

Feeling strange and uneasy, she went back to the table and found that the tome had opened to the diagram of the library. She studied the page, finding it hard to follow the spidery lines, as mold obscured most of them. She wiped an area gently with the corner of a napkin, but it only smeared and made it more difficult to read.

"Mrs. Granger might know how to clean off mold," she said to herself. She got the oddest sensation, as if someone were staring at her, and turned around quickly. No one had entered the room. She never should have listened to Mr. Ripple and his fancy notions that the house was haunted.

Captain Brooks wiped his hand across his forehead. Creating a minor rain cloud was a challenge. He'd need to work on some of the effects; but those things took time to master. Making things out of pure energy demanded concentration and dedication. He'd always been short on both, but was getting better all the time.

What pleased and excited him was that Cassie had found the old tome and took interest in the account. He'd always known she could figure out about the treasure if she dug deeper into the history of Fairweather.

He flew across the room in pure excitement and his movement fluttered the pages. People around here were finally beginning to notice him! What a stroke of luck that Mr. Ripple had moved in. *He'll see things my way,* Captain Brooks said to himself, *and I can get some results—after all these years!*

He kicked his heels together and hovered in the ceiling right above Cassie's head. For someone so clever, she did have her slow spots. Not believing in ghosts was ignorant. If she'd only open her eyes, she'd be able to see ghosts everywhere. It was as crowded as any great thoroughfare of London, but clearly she had her blinders on, like a common horse.

It would change, though. He would make sure of it.

Cassie could've sworn she heard a tapping sound in the ceiling and the distant sound of laughter. The men must be sharing some fond memories, she thought, and peered out into the hallway. But she heard only silence. The men had left the study. The door stood open, and wind blew down the hallway from the study.

She hurried across the room to shut the window. The rain had stopped as abruptly as it started, and the sun already tinted the edges of the clouds with bright gold.

The room smelled of sherry and cigars and that elusive male scent, somewhat rough and abrasive, that both excited her and rubbed her the wrong way.

She'd never thought of the effect Dylan's scent would have on her senses. She couldn't recall having had any reaction to James one way or the other.

She decided to open the window again.

The tome had shown the diagram of the study, and she studied the walls for any indication of cracks. She looked carefully around the fireplace, but the stones that had been used and the carved mantelpiece looked tight and undisturbed.

The built-in bookcases on each side of the fireplace seemed as solid as the day they were built. Fortunately, the wood had held up well over the centuries, one of the few things that hadn't decayed, except for the flaking paint.

Just as she started going over the walls with the flat of her hand, the door opened. She threw a glance over her shoulder and saw Dylan. He'd tossed off his coat and loosened his cravat as if ready for some kind of work.

"I helped Ned and Mr. Ripple carry the trunks upstairs. Eddie is traveling with as much luggage as a debutante going to her first Season." He walked over to the table and downed the last of the sherry in his glass.

"It would've been courteous to let us know he was coming for a visit," she said with some asperity, but kept looking for clues on the wall.

"I didn't know he was coming. He has no fondness for the countryside. I hadn't the faintest idea he'd been struck by Cupid's arrow—with Giselle Duggan, no less."

" 'Tis my opinion they'll make a strange couple," she mused out loud. "That is if Mr. Duggan approves of the match, which I doubt."

"Strange couples are sometimes the most interesting," he said, "and Eddie is a very persistent man even if his causes are sometimes dubious."

He was standing right behind her. His breath fanned her neck gently, and she grew unaccountably warm.

"What are you doing, Cassie? Staring at the wall as some kind of punishment?"

She could not help but laugh. "You have a certain flair with words. Maybe my staring at the wall brings back memories from your school days. If I recall, James claimed you had some wild years."

He barked a laugh. "You have to remember that James went ahead of us, but I'm sure he divulged very little about his school years. He was sent down a couple of times, did you know that?"

"What James did doesn't interest me."

"I suppose Cupid's arrow didn't touch you when you saw him for the first time?"

His sweet breath kept wafting against her neck, and she had difficulty thinking. She refused to answer, but of course James had not inspired any tender feelings within her.

"What exactly *are* you doing, Cassie?"

"I'm looking for double walls or secret rooms,"

she said. "It's all in the account that Captain Brooks wrote as he built Fairweather."

"And you believe there might be secrets in the secret rooms?"

"You never know what may be hidden."

"Chests of treasure from the seven seas?" he asked with heavy sarcasm.

"It wouldn't be the first time old things have been found—in the strangest places."

"You're right, as always." He placed his hands on her shoulders, and she could feel the heat from his skin through the thin material of her gown.

She wanted to move away, but couldn't. "Does it irk you?"

"What? That you're always right?" His breath warmed her ear now, and she stood mesmerized.

She nodded, unable to breathe properly.

"At least you don't lack self-confidence." His voice had grown softer and more intimate.

"Anyone with . . . any sense could see . . . the practicality of my . . . views," she said, losing her concentration. His male scent overwhelmed her to a point where she lost all coherent thought, and the wall in front of her eyes became a blur.

"Always," he whispered. "When I need a conscience, I'll come to you. You will always set me on the right course."

"Somehow that sounds so unflattering." She put a steadying hand on the wall in front of her. "Like a stern moralist."

"An elderly stern moralist," he murmured against her ear. "Which you aren't. At your age it's good to let go to life and enjoy some immoral pleasures, but I'd bet you don't know the first thing about how to relish life."

"I don't bet," she replied, stiffening.

"That's why I'd win. I bet all the time, and I like to live my life on the edge with lots of excitement."

She stiffened even more and took a deep breath. Moving away from his hands, which had rested on her shoulders, she walked quickly toward the door. When she turned around, he was smiling from ear to ear. A teasing glint sparked in his eyes, and she felt a spurt of anger that he'd gotten the better of her.

She straightened her back and gave him a steady stare. "I'd bet *you* that you're not man enough to stand up to the challenge of Fairweather. It takes time, backbone, and dedication—things you don't have."

"I'm never one to turn down a bet, no matter how challenging," he said. "But you have no stake to put up, do you?"

Thoughts raced through her mind. She had nothing to stake. *Nothing.*

"If I win, you'll have to make a public apology to all of my friends at the gathering I will host to celebrate the accomplished renovations."

She didn't have to think about it. "Very well. I accept the challenge."

Six

The next morning Hazel Elderberry came fluttering into the dining room where Cassie had taken refuge from the commotion of Mr. Edward Bunney's presence. He brought a tempest wherever he went.

One could hear him clear across the gardens, or from the upstairs as he held discourse with the long-suffering Mr. Ripple. All he ever talked about was the celestial blue eyes and angel-soft hair of Miss Duggan.

After two days, Cassie was getting tired of his romantic outpourings.

"Cassie, I saw a man lurking in the garden. I think he was trying to get in the side door, the one that is locked at all times, seeing as the key is missing."

"A man lurking? Did you get a good look at him?"

Hazel shook her head. "No, but he was wearing a dark suit of clothes, like a man of business or a higher servant."

Cassie frowned. "Why would he be *lurking* in the middle of the afternoon?"

"Mayhap he's connected to the baby boy somehow. The father?"

"Hmm, that's a possibility." Cassie got up and peered through the window.

"When he saw me, he hurried off without as much as a 'good afternoon.' He had his hat pulled low over his ears."

Cassie knew it was useless to look for him, but she scanned the backyard anyway, seeing only Mr. Bunney shading his eyes as he stared in the direction of Duggan's property. She wondered if he'd noticed anyone.

"Was Mr. Bunney outside when you saw the man, Hazel?"

The older woman shook her head. "No, I didn't see anyone. I was taking my strengthening walk with Hermione who complained about my quick stride all the way." Her face took on a mutinous expression. "Sometimes Hermione can be annoyingly talkative."

Cassie thought of the meek Hermione and silently saluted her for daring to rebel against Hazel's tyranny in any way. "You can't be together constantly without some conflict," she said blandly.

"What Hermione would do without me I don't know," Hazel said, her frown deepening. "Without guidance, she would lie abed all day long."

Cassie had a sharp comment on the tip of her tongue but refrained from blurting it out. She would gain nothing from pointing out that Hermione was surely capable of taking care of herself. She stared down at the old tome that lay open on the table in front of her. It intrigued her more than she ever thought possible.

"You're still reading that ancient book?" Hazel asked and peered over Cassie's shoulder at the fragile pages. "I wouldn't have the patience to decipher Captain Brooks's spidery handwriting. The man must've felt self-important to have written such a lengthy account of himself."

"He had no problems with confidence," Cassie said. "But what is true in here and what is heresy is hard to know. He describes all parts of Fairweather, but many of the building's details can't be verified. They are simply missing."

"Renovations obviously have been done over the centuries," Hazel said, "but I have to say the last generation—Dylan's parents—were apparently neglectful. I'm willing to bet they didn't sink one groat into the upkeep, which is a pity."

"They had no interest in the history of the estate," Cassie said, "or these old books would not have been buried in the attic."

"But you do." Hazel gave Cassie a long glance. "You're the only one who cares about Fairweather. It should rightfully be yours. You are a Wenthaven, after all, indirectly part of the Brooks family."

Cassie felt an unfamiliar longing squeeze her heart as if Hazel had touched some deep part she herself hadn't been aware of. "Everyone wants a place to call their own," she said noncommittally. "I always lived at the parsonage, at the mercy of the Church, and Father's calling was his flock. He never thought to build anything for himself."

"When Father died at the young age of ninety, we were thrust upon the world," Hazel said. "I found it very selfish of him to leave us when we had nowhere to go."

Cassie could not stop herself from laughing. "You think he chose to leave when he did?"

Hazel looked mutinous. "He *abandoned* us."

Cassie saw the futility of continuing that line of conversation. "What do you think of Mr. Bunney's chances of finding true love with Giselle?"

Hazel took on an air of importance as she sat down

next to Cassie. "Hermione and I are going to help him, you know. We shall smooth his path to true love."

"How, if I may enquire? You are no closer to the Duggans than I am. In fact, we tend to avoid each other as a rule."

" 'Tis never too late to cultivate a friendship," Hazel said.

Cassie had no idea how that could be accomplished, since Mr. Duggan ruled his household with an iron fist and showed nothing but hostility toward Fairweather's occupants.

"I'm sure Mr. Duggan is a reasonable man if you look closely enough," Hazel continued. "We'll just have to convince him that Miss Duggan would be fortunate to have Mr. Bunney as her prime suitor."

Cassie refrained from uttering her opinion, as she desired peace at all costs. Hazel had the personality of a terrier, and Cassie wondered if Mr. Duggan would be inclined to aim one of his rifles at the old lady when she confronted him. "I pray you don't do anything foolhardy, Hazel."

"Hmph! I feel Mr. Bunney has been treated unfairly. Just imagine having your arm pierced because you put your cloak over the mud to protect Miss Duggan."

"He did more than that, Hazel."

"All in the course of preventing Miss Duggan from pain."

"Be that as it may, Mr. Duggan took a dim view of the incident, and I'm convinced he would be horrified to know—which he probably does by now—that Mr. Bunney is staying with us."

"We shall have to talk some sense into him," Hazel said with conviction. "It's all there is to it."

Cassie rose from the table and gathered her reading material in a hurry. "I must see if Mrs. Granger needs my help with the baby."

Before Hazel could utter her opinion about the orphan's situation, Cassie fled from the room.

Two hours later she searched the walls for hidden doors in the upstairs hallway. It was rapidly becoming an obsession, and she felt frustrated at her lack of progress. *Somewhere* there had to be a clue. And who knew what she might find in the secret hiding place?

Captain Brooks had left too many hints that he'd planned to hide a treasure for her to ignore the whole thing. What if she found riches that might be enough to fund the repairs of the estate? A farfetched idea, but not impossible after what she'd read in the old tome.

Dylan came up the stairs dressed in riding clothes, his hair windblown and his eyes sparkling with vigor. Evidently he'd been exercising his horse without a thought to the fate of Fairweather. She glanced away as heat rose in her cheeks. It irked her no end that she couldn't stay indifferent to him.

"Cassie, you look lovely as ever," he said, a hint of teasing in his voice. He stopped in front of her, but she averted her eyes.

"Good morning," she said crisply.

"Again I find you staring at the walls. It's not part of your duties as steward. I think I mentioned something about clearing out the weeds and the brush."

"Ned and his nephews have been working on it, and I'm personally weeding the herb and vegetable gardens, but delving into the history of Fairweather could be just as important if I find what I'm looking for." She wished for a moment she hadn't opened her mouth.

"You mean the hidden doors? Are you saying there might be more to that?" He braced one hand against the water-stained wallpaper and looked down into her eyes.

She couldn't turn away from his penetrating blue gaze. "Yes . . . I suspect Captain Brooks put away something he didn't want the world to find during his time. Perhaps it was loot that would destroy him if it were discovered."

"Loot?"

"As in hidden treasure. We know there's a mystery to be solved, if Mrs. Granger is to be believed. We also know there's a feud between the Duggans and the Brooks, but we don't know why."

"The Duggans always were seafarers at an earlier time—or pirates, if you want to use a less flattering term. Perhaps there existed a friendship between the two families at one time, but something went seriously awry."

"If we discover the treasure, I believe we'll find out what truly happened in the past. But why would an age-old feud be upheld today?"

Dylan shrugged his shoulders. "I know Duggan hasn't gotten along with anyone in my family, and when Seffington took over the deed of the estate, the acrimony increased tenfold. I doubt Duggan or Seffington have many friends as it is."

"Do you believe in the possibility of a treasure?" she asked.

Dylan tapped his fingertips on the wall. "I doubt there is one. I believe in more tangible opportunities, as in winning a large sum of money at Newmarket."

Anger rose hot and trembling in her chest. "James used to say the same old words, and he always lost."

"James is not me," he said sharply. "James never

looked beyond the surface. As far as I know, he was too lazy to plot any strategy, and that's why he got killed in the war."

"You're condemning your own brother."

"But I'm telling the truth, however ruthless. I may be a gambler, but I'm not selfish to a point where I don't care about how my actions will touch those around me."

His words affected Cassie deeply. James had cared about no one but himself. "I suppose you thought about that when you fathered the little orphaned boy," she said, the words slipping out before she had a chance to stop them.

His eyes blazed with sudden anger. "Is that an accusation?" he asked between clenched teeth.

She shook her head, feeling utterly foolish. "An observation," she said defensively. "There's no denying the babe has your eyes, and the Wenthaven silver rattle."

"I resent your looking down your nose and throwing around accusations that have no foundation in reality. I have done absolutely nothing to earn your scorn. In fact, it's due to my generosity that you and your protégés are still here." He slapped his thigh with his folded gloves and stared at her, his whole body tense.

"I apologize," she said meekly. "They are naught but accusations, and it was excessively rude of me to speak."

He seemed to let out his breath a little at a time, then inhaled deeply. For a moment she thought he would explode, but he controlled his temper admirably. She felt weak at the knees and a tremble went up her spine. Never had such a feeling of foolishness come over her.

"By Jupiter, I never knew the depths of your animosity."

She wasn't sure if he meant gambling or James. "Animosity?"

"Toward gambling, mostly. I can understand if you never had a tender spot for James."

" 'Tis obvious *you* didn't," she said.

He looked away, a troubled expression in his eyes. "James treated me with a wealth of scorn. He was a lot older than Dermott and I. We didn't have a lot in common."

Certainly not temperament, Cassie thought. She suspected Dylan might use the words "cold fish" to describe James.

She noticed the light in the hallway had darkened considerably. The sky outside had turned leaden, and the wind had increased to great force. The windows rattled with the fury of it. Before she could speak, rain started pouring, splashing against the windows as the wind drove across the Channel.

"Oh, no. We'd better bring out the buckets. This is a furious storm."

He glanced toward the window and frowned. "Buckets?"

"When it rains this hard, the leaks in the roof will make themselves known. It happens quite often." Mumbling an excuse, she hurried away. Besides having to tend to the emergency at hand, she couldn't stay in his presence any longer.

Three hours later, they were emptying all ten buckets and pans that had served to catch the dripping water. Cassie's brow was covered with perspiration and her dress clung to her back. Everyone was helping to mop up the spills on the floor—except Mr. Bunney, who surveyed the room which he'd been allotted. He stood in the open doorway with a mournful expression on his face.

"I will forever whip myself that my arm is out of commission. There's much I could've done to aid the situation," he said to Dylan, who had rolled up his shirtsleeves and was wiping down the wall, where a rivulet of water had spread out into a myriad of tiny streams.

"What would you have done?" Dylan asked grimly. He watched as Cassie carried a pan of water across the room.

"I would've climbed to the roof and patched the leaks," Mr. Bunney said matter-of-factly.

Cassie threw an incredulous glance at Dylan, who could only laugh.

"Eddie, I'm eternally grateful for your concern, but I have difficulty picturing you in pouring rain with boards, hammer, and nails. First of all, just think of the damage your shiny Hessian boots would sustain."

"I would never wear my Hessians to do work like that," Mr. Bunney said with scorn. "My topboots would do nicely. Or I could've sent Ripple upstairs. He's a wizard with any kind of tool, aren't you Ripple?"

The valet raised his chin and pinched his lips into a thin line. "My *forte* runs rather in the line of shaving tools, needle, and thread," he said rather huffily.

"Don't be so modest," Mr. Bunney said. He held the door that was already open for Cassie as she walked through with the pan.

Dylan glanced at the huge wet patches in the ceiling and felt a desire to run away. This looked more than grim. It looked impossible. "The first thing that has to be repaired is the roof. Fact is, it has to be replaced."

"You're taking on a great challenge, my friend," Mr. Bunney said.

"I know. I'm not sure I want to take it on. I'm thinking about it," Dylan said. He heard Cassie's light step as she came back into the room. She must have heard his statement, but she made no indication.

"I don't envy you the task," Mr. Bunney said. "I surely would not want it. I'm going to win Giselle's hand, and then I'm going back to London. Rusticating in the country can be wearing."

"I'm never bored in the country," Cassie said. "There's always something to do, something beautiful to see."

"I don't care for those birds that bicker at five in the morning, and I don't know one species of flower from the other. All those trees waving in the breeze don't interest me."

No one replied, but Ripple made an audible sniff as if in agreement.

"Not to mention the offense to my delicate nose," Mr. Bunney said softly, almost to himself.

"I daresay the smells in London are just as overpowering as they are in the country," Dylan said. "At least there are some sweet scents from the flowers here."

"They make me sneeze," Mr. Bunney said peevishly. "If I'm not careful, I shall be laid low with inflammation of the lungs." He straightened his waistcoat and touched the immaculate fall of his neckcloth. "I need to make haste in courting Miss Duggan." He glanced around the pitiful room. "If circumstances were different, we could plan a gath-

ering here at Fairweather, any excuse to invite Miss
Duggan to attend."

"Yes, but I don't think Miss Duggan would be im-
pressed by this environment."

"Hmm." Mr. Bunney pressed a fingertip against
his chin. "Do we know anyone in the area, Dylan?"

"Someone with a magnificent estate?" Dylan
asked, cringing at the truth of his own financial circumstances. He glanced at his friend, who didn't notice.

Cassie noticed, though, and he saw a fleeting moment of compassion in her eyes. That brief second
soothed him, and he swallowed hard. She understood
what it felt like to have nothing. Not that Eddie had
very much, Dylan thought, but the man always saw
himself marrying into money. Dylan had never
planned that far; no young damsel had caught his
interest. The Marriage Mart did just fine without him.
He detested the old dowagers and chaperones looking
down their noses at his humble status. It didn't matter
that Lord Seffington had been his grandfather. The
old man had left nothing in his will to bolster Dylan's
estate.

"I'd say we call on someone in the near future,"
Mr. Bunney said, breaking into Dylan's reverie.
"There are any number of peers who boast estates
in Sussex."

"You're free to stay with any one of them," Dylan
said.

"But you're my friend," Mr. Bunney protested. "I
know I can always have a place with you."

Water dripped from the ceiling and hit Dylan in
the face. He wiped it off and wondered if the whole
ceiling would come down over their heads. "For a

while anyway," he replied. "As long as I have a roof over my head."

"You always were a soul of generosity, Dylan. Of all my friends, you're the one who cares the most." Mr. Bunney turned to Cassie. "The man has a heart of gold. All his friends will attest to that."

"Gold? I'm surprised he hasn't gambled it away," Cassie said brazenly, and Mr. Bunney took a step back.

The barb hurt Dylan, but he steeled himself against her accusing stare. It didn't come, however. As had happened earlier, she looked guilty and her cheeks blossomed red.

"I'm sorry," she said almost inaudibly.

Seven

The following day Dylan made a decision. He couldn't stay here doing nothing, and he had no funds to do anything worthwhile. What he needed was a large sum of money so that he could replace the roof at Fairweather. Without a solid roof, there was no hope for any other renovations to succeed.

He turned to his friend, who was sitting in a frayed wing chair across from him in the library, nursing a brandy snifter. "Eddie, I have to go back to London to earn some funds. What do you say? Let's go today."

Mr. Bunney looked troubled. "Today? What about Miss Duggan, the Fairest of Fair?"

"She's not going anywhere. We'll be back in a week or less. It would do you good to get some distance. All this pining is never good for a fellow."

"We're not making any progress," Mr. Bunney moaned.

"Well, you can't walk up and knock on the front door, can you? If you could, there wouldn't be a problem."

"I had high hopes you would be close friends with the Duggans."

"That will never happen, so you might as well put

it out of your mind. We'll have to come up with some other strategy for your courtship."

"The courtship may be doomed before it even starts," Mr. Bunney said gloomily.

"Where's your sense of adventure?" Dylan got up and walked around the dilapidated room. The heel of his boot snagged a threadbare spot in the carpet and ripped it. A curse hung on his lips. "I've got to do something or go mad," he snapped. "The truth is, I have to prove to myself that I can create something of value."

Mr. Bunney patted his wounded arm. "I'll go with you, but don't expect me to be of any help."

Dylan gave him a long look. "You can always stay here and take embroidery lessons from the Elderberry twins. That's fine by me."

Mr. Bunney heaved himself out of the chair with sudden haste. "I can be on the road within the hour! I'll have Ripple pack a few clean shirts and we'll be off."

Dylan went in search of Cassie to tell her of his plans. He found her on her hands and knees in the vegetable garden, pulling out weeds. A long streak of mud ran across her cheek, and he wanted to wipe it off, but restrained himself.

She got up and brushed off her skirt. He noticed the frayed hem and felt an urge to buy her ten new dresses, but he knew her pride would prevent her from accepting anything from him.

"I'm going back to London for a few days."

Silence hung dense between them as he sensed her unspoken accusation. She must have sensed his plans for acquiring some money without heavy toil.

"Meanwhile, I would appreciate it if you can look

after things here. The more we clear the grounds, the easier it'll be to start the repairs on the house."

"You have a point," she said, studying the thick vegetation that still flourished despite Ned's efforts. "I shall ask Ned to bring more members of his family to deal with the job. The good point is that they'll not be opposed to taking their wages in increments."

"I have every intention of paying them for their work," Dylan said tersely. Her lack of faith touched him on the raw, and she had a way of making him look at his previous life as a great spread of wasteland. She had no right to accuse him, loudly or silently.

She didn't say anything, but her silence spoke volumes. Her brown eyes held a hint of sadness. She wiped her forearm across her cheek, smearing the mud even more.

He could not stop himself from reaching out and cleaning the mud away with one gentle swipe of his finger. He expected her to jerk away, but she didn't.

"I take my work seriously," she said. "When you return, the brush will be cleared away, and the weeds will all be gone."

He glanced at the garden. "I'm sure they will." He wanted to pull her into his arms and hold her, but knew it was out of the question.

He rolled his beaver hat between his hands. "Well . . . I'll be back."

She gave a little wave. "Godspeed."

She didn't wish him good luck.

One hour and several arguments later about the two trunks Mr. Bunney wanted to bring, they set off— without the trunks.

Dylan turned around in the saddle and glanced at Fairweather. It held an air of tranquility in the sunlight, which also revealed every flaw of the old mansion. Still, Fairweather was his. For the first time, he felt a small sense of pride. He could bring the place back to life.

Cassie tossed and turned in her bed that night, plagued with bad dreams. An unseasonable cold enveloped the house, and she shivered awake and found she'd tossed off the old quilts that served to keep her warm.

She sat up in bed and righted her nightgown, which had twisted around her. Something seemed to hover in the shadows, but she couldn't make out anything in the weak moonlight coming through the windows.

"This is silliness," she said out loud to dismiss the feeling of unease. "I'm becoming fanciful." *It's the house's fault,* she thought. Fairweather had a life of its own, and lots of secrets. She lay back against the pillows and wondered why she'd become so obsessed with revealing those secrets. Every day since she'd found the written account of Fairweather, she'd been searching for secret hiding places. She *had* to find out if the account was true.

She pulled the quilts to her chin and closed her eyes in an effort to go back to sleep. One hour later found her still awake. She couldn't get over the sensation someone was in the room with her, watching.

As fear started to get the better of her, she got up and lighted the candles by the bed. All looked ordinary, just as it always did. No monsters skulked in the corners ready to pounce on her.

"This is really strange," she said to herself as the hairs on her arms and neck rose. A cold draft rolled across the room, and she was surprised the weather had changed so much. Surely it couldn't be this cold outside.

The coldness filled the entire room with uneasiness, and for the first time she wondered if the ghost stories were true. She'd felt the cold before, but had associated it with the cool breeze from the sea seeping through the cracks in the building. The feeling she got now was one of force, as if something were pushing at her, not so much physically, but urging her to pay attention.

Glancing around the room, she fought an urge to flee. There was no ghost. Captain Brooks had long gone—hundreds of years ago, in fact. She didn't know if pirates went to heaven, but left he had.

Captain Brooks snorted through his thin nostrils. Such an obstinate woman. Intelligence she had, but it was a pity she remained so bullheaded. Faugh, but he detested stubborn women! His Elinor had been one of the worst. He never could talk any sense into her.

He hovered for a moment over Cassie's head, trying to figure out how to reveal the journal to her. It had been hidden for many a year, so many years there might be only dust left of it. He'd not been able to catch anyone's attention in the previous century. They had all been a self-absorbed and ignorant lot, he thought scornfully.

He maneuvered all of his energy into the built-in armoire. He'd been excessively proud of that piece of craftsmanship, with its elegant carvings around the doors and the delicate wrought-iron hinges. What the wood needed was care, some oil to bring back the luster.

He dived in between Cassie's few dresses and fluttered above the rack, searching for the false panel right over the door opening. It hid a small space which had held his journal for all this time. No one had found it during his lifetime. He'd made sure of that.

Putting all his concentration into opening the unobtrusive door, he felt exhausted. Focusing took every ounce of strength he had, and he grew ever more delicate.

If he weren't careful, he'd turn into nothing but a feeble wisp with no power whatsoever. If only the people would cooperate some, things wouldn't be so onerous. The disbelievers were the worst kind. At least he had an ally in Mr. Ripple, who was hoping to catch a glimpse of the Fairweather ghost. He would catch more than that if Cassie proved to be too hard a nut to crack.

It was time for the whole truth to come out.

Captain Brooks wiped his forehead, finding little substance. That troubled him. In his heyday, he'd been a power to be reckoned with, but these days he ran on spare energy. He had to accomplish his mission before it was too late. Things had to be set right if he would ever be able to redeem himself. He'd been humbled enough hovering between two worlds like this. Over time, he'd seen the errors of his ways, and he had this one chance to change the past.

With a mighty burst of energy, he opened the door and let the journal fall to the floor in the closet. Cassie would hear the thump. She was awake, her senses on full alert—she sensed his presence, though her mind fought the knowledge tooth and nail.

He moved back into the bedroom to watch her reaction.

Cassie heard the thud on the floor and started. Her heart began to pound and ice flowed through her veins. If she could see no one in her room, why did she feel as if someone stood right beside her? She wrapped her arms around her middle as cold enveloped her, and she debated whether to investigate what had fallen in the armoire.

Her heart hammering, she grabbed the brass candlestick from her nightstand. In the worst case, it could always be used as a weapon.

Her knees like rubber, she walked to the armoire and opened the door. At first she saw nothing but her familiar row of dresses. They looked even more dilapidated than ever, as if they'd hung there for two hundred years as part of the house.

"Something will have to happen to change my fortune," she said to herself. She had considered taking up a position as a governess, but the thought didn't much appeal to her. It still might be her only way out.

She lifted the candlestick to take a better look at the inside of the armoire and immediately noticed the old book lying on top of her shoes. She'd never seen it before. Somehow it must've fallen, but she had no idea how.

Peering into the darkness, she glanced around, seeing nothing out of the ordinary. No one lurked in the closet, but the fact that the book had somehow entered the armoire could not be explained.

"I'll have to take a good look tomorrow," she whispered to herself. Still shaking, she retrieved the old book and went back to her bed. The uneasy feeling lingered, but peace was creeping in and the wind had quieted down outside.

She had a feeling if she spoke out loud to the room, she would get an answer. That's how strongly she sensed the presence of something alive. Jumping back into bed, she pulled the covers up to her chin and plumped the pillows behind her head.

Curious despite her fear, she started looking through the book. *Journal,* it read in spidery letters, *by Captain Fortunatus Brooks, anno 1665.* He'd written this during the last year of his life.

One hundred and fifty years had passed since he put down his final entry in the journal, she thought as she flipped through the papery and powdery vellum. If she weren't careful, the whole tome would fall apart.

"Captain Brooks," she said out loud, "I should've known you would be involved somehow."

Despite herself, she held her breath and listened to the silence. Glancing at the shadows in the corners, she half expected the pirate captain from the portrait, now wearing a curly black wig, frilled shirt, and red satin coat with embroidered facings to step forward, but no one made himself known. The only thing alive was the finger-thin drafts of cold air wisping across the room from the windows.

She shook her head at her own foolishness and started reading the handwriting she knew so well by now. Captain Brooks had been meticulous in keeping records.

This personal journal had a different tone than the other account. If she hadn't been so skittish, she would've continued reading, but she laid the book aside and slid down on the pillows.

As soon as she closed her eyes, she thought she heard strange sounds, and her eyelids flew open. It would be futile to try to sleep.

When the birds finally started singing and dawn crept rosy over the hills, she fell into a fitful slumber.

Captain Brooks used another burst of energy to blow his journal open to a specific page. This was all he could do. The rest was up to Cassie. With a deep sigh, he repaired to the attic, where hopefully he could restore his energy just in case it was needed once more.

Eight

Dylan looked at the men around the card tables at Watier's club in London and wondered if his face held that same avid look, his eyes the same fever of excitement. A young baronet unaccustomed to the hard, calculating world of gambling had just lost ten thousand pounds at the faro tables.

" 'Pon rep, if someone doesn't caution that greenhorn, he'll be in River Tick by morning," Edward Bunney said to Dylan.

Dylan nodded. "His uncle is with him, but I'm not sure of his capability to lead the young man away from disaster."

"You could probably make an easy gain there," Eddie said speculatively.

"You know I could never take advantage of someone that young and innocent. I win my funds honorably against equal adversaries. 'Tis the only way."

"You always set high standards." Eddie grinned and clapped Dylan's shoulder. "That's why I call you my friend, and I'm honored to have you as my friend."

Dylan should've been cheered by the words. At one time he would've been, but today something had gone out of the pleasure of gambling. His vision had changed. It was as if he were looking at the gambling tables through Cassie's eyes, the ones that condemned because gambling was not honorable work.

Still, it took great concentration and strategy to be a good gambler, skills that had taken a lot of time for him to acquire.

He reveled in brilliant strategy. Maybe he should've bought a pair of colors and gone across the Channel to fight the French. No, at heart he couldn't face violence and death.

"You already won five hundred pounds tonight from Captain Lewis, Dylan. That ought to cheer you some."

Dylan made a grimace. Nothing cheered him tonight. "I need at least two thousand pounds to start any significant repairs. I need a lot more than that, but I don't need to procure the whole amount in one night."

"Not that you couldn't," Eddie said.

"Under the right circumstances."

Together they sat down in the armchairs arranged along the wall and ordered a bottle of claret.

"If you could win twenty thousand pounds, you wouldn't have to gamble again," Eddie mused aloud.

Dylan gave him an incredulous look. "You must have windmills in your head. For me to win that much would mean total ruin for someone else."

"You wouldn't have to win it all from one person."

Dylan stared morosely at the hazard table in the corner. The dice rattled in the leather cups, and gamblers held their breaths as the dice rolled. He couldn't understand what was wrong with him. All he could think of was Cassie and Fairweather, in that order. At times he was even thinking about the weather there, the fresh breezes and the sparkling waters of the Channel.

He could feel Eddie staring at him. He returned the penetrating stare reluctantly. Fortunately, the bottle of claret arrived with two glasses and they savored the first sip.

"You've changed, Dylan."

"No, I have not."

Eddie heaved an exasperated sigh. "If Lord Brockton arrives, you'll have your chance at whist," Eddie said. "I heard he won a large purse last night at Brooks's. A huge sum, in fact."

"That old roué wins a large sum and loses one all in the same night," Dylan said. "For all we know, he might've lost it already tonight."

"With your glum outlook, winning tonight seems remote," Eddie said hotly. "I spend agonizing time away from my Beloved to please you, and all you can do is complain and throw mournful looks into your wineglass. It's the outside of enough!"

"I didn't use to be saddled with all this responsibility," Dylan said defensively.

"And you hadn't looked into Cassie's brown eyes," Eddie said shrewdly. "I have a feeling I'm not the only one who wants to return to Fairweather posthaste."

"Plague take it, Eddie, that's pure fabrication on your part. Just because you've been struck by Cupid's arrow doesn't mean I have, too. You see everything through the haze of love. It clouds reason."

"And a good thing it is," Eddie replied. "You could use a bit of romance in your life after all the difficulties you went through in the last year, with both James and Dermott turning up their toes, and Seffington to boot."

Dylan couldn't reply as he thought of the tragedies that had struck the family, but he'd held it together emotionally most of the time. He'd thrown himself into the whirlpool of activity that was London and tried to keep his distance from the pain.

It had crept up on him late at night, when he had to face himself alone. He had wandered that dark alley of desolation many a night, but light was filtering through at last.

" 'Tis part of life to lose the people you care about," he said and sipped the claret. "You move forward somehow, even if you limp along. You have to move forward or be destroyed. There's no choice."

" 'Sfaith, but you're getting too deep for me, old fellow."

Dylan laughed. " 'Tis that time of night when things get really deep. When the naked truth will out and you can't hide behind polite façades any longer."

"And things get ugly?" Eddie pointed at one of the card tables where a heated argument was under way. "We have a challenge brewing here. Pistols at dawn, no doubt. Which one are you going to bet on? The moonling in the ridiculous cravat or the cawker with the Byron curls? He has the highest shirtpoints I've ever seen. Just for that he ought to be called out."

Dylan chuckled as he viewed the young man of fashion. The argument was about cheating at cards, but Dylan doubted any cheating had been going on. They were too incompetent for that.

Their voices rose as the anger intensified, and before long the cawker with the shirtpoints had applied his glove to the moonling's cheek. He didn't doubt there would be a duel at dawn at Barn Elms. Such a waste—all to satisfy someone's stiff pride.

"You're fortunate, Eddie, that Mr. Duggan didn't run you through the heart."

Eddie straightened himself and took on a defensive air. " 'Tis not as if I'm completely without fencing skills, or aptitude. I don't have an interest in jumping around with a sharp blade and waving it at other people, so I don't practice much. I much more prefer a comfortable chair with a glass of claret at my elbow—like tonight." He took a deep swallow of the wine and smacked his lips.

"You never had an interest in athletic pursuits, Eddie."

"Be that as it may, I'd do anything for my Beloved Giselle. *Anything.* Even if I have to take on every one of my enemies at Gentleman Jackson's boxing parlor."

"You would be pounded to a pulp, Eddie," Dylan said, feeling drained. All he wanted to do was crawl into bed and forget he was in London, but that would not pay for any repairs at Fairweather.

He'd never felt this kind of reluctance or actual *boredom* in the capital. A good game had always made his blood sing, and the noisy crowds in the streets and in the gaming hells had made him feel right at home.

Eddie nudged his arm. "Lord Brockton just walked in, and he looks like the cat that got into the cream. I'd say he's got deep pockets tonight."

Dylan glanced across the room, assessing his adversary. He'd gone many rounds with Brockton in the past. Some he'd won and some he'd lost. You never knew with Brockton. "You may be right, and I'd say he's three sheets to the wind." For a moment he felt the old sap rising, but it abated as soon as it had started.

"You'll win what you need tonight, and then we can return to Fairweather and the dazzling Giselle," Eddie said.

Dylan set down his wineglass and stood. Brockton noticed his presence and waved. A smile lit his face, and challenge glittered in his eyes. Brockton never shirked a confrontation. He reveled in it. Dylan knew it would be difficult to win tonight.

Even as the evening lengthened into night, Cassie could not sleep. Sitting with the Hazel and Hermione, she'd been totally absorbed reading the journal Captain Brooks had left behind and had discovered a fascination with it she didn't think possible. Here were all the accounts of his travels and what he'd gained personally, in joy and in sorrow.

She set down the book on her lap, smoothed out the folds of her lavender gown, and righted the lace fichu at her neck. She stared out the window, where moonlight streamed strong and silvery across the darkness, making the grounds into a fairy landscape.

She looked over at Hazel, who snoozed in the other wing chair, and Hermione, whose head was falling sideways as she sat in the rickety sofa along the wall. Hazel awoke with a start.

"What was that?" she asked groggily.

"What?" Cassie asked.

"That moaning sound."

Cassie drew her eyebrows together. "I didn't hear anything."

"You never do, but I'm positive it's that dreadful ghost that clumps around at night."

"You're too fanciful, Hazel. Have you ever seen it?"

Hazel touched her bun and attached a stray wisp of hair. "No. I don't have the second sight. But in that moment before awakening, I see something, and I hear that moaning noise—as if someone has eaten too much rum cake."

"I've never seen anything, but after reading some of Captain Brooks's journal, I wouldn't be surprised if his soul failed to find peace. Eating too much rum cake would not have been his main problem."

"Your hands are green from the weeds," Hazel said absentmindedly.

Cassie studied her roughened and stained hands with concern. "They are, aren't they? But it's not as if I'm going to society balls or other events where I have to present an elegant picture. No one but you will notice my hands."

"Dylan will."

"Pooh! And if he does, who cares?"

"You act indifferent, but you care."

Cassie admitted silently that she did care, but dismissed the thought immediately. "Anyway, Captain Brooks's fleet of ships successfully did twenty-five raids, some of them evidently very lucrative. The fleet—or what was left of it—ended up disbanding eventually, and Captain Brooks docked his ship *Juanita* in Brighton, which was naught but a small fishing town in those days. He brought home a slew of riches."

"Harum-scarum character no doubt," Hazel mused. "He had a lot of gall to plunder the innocent wayfarers of the sea."

"He went to the Indian Ocean, the West Indies, China, and the Mediterranean. He wrote highly of Egypt, where he actually spent some time on terra firma."

"Egypt is too far from home, and for all the money in the world I would not have wanted to sail all those foreign seas and encounter those slanted-eyed Easterners—or the Moors. They would've stricken dread in my heart."

Cassie smiled. "Where's your sense of adventure, Hazel?"

"Adventure is for fools and young people. I'm content with my embroidery and a warm hearth." She paused for a moment. "If I had my only wish, it would be for more company, preferably from London."

"So you could gossip," Cassie filled in.

Hazel took on a mutinous expression. "There's no reason to tease me, Cassie. I admit, however, that I thoroughly enjoyed the event of Mr. Bunney's arrival. He brought a whiff of fresh air to these sedate parts of Sussex."

"He certainly did."

Hazel set down her embroidery hoop and gazed intently at Cassie. "In fact, Hermione and I have been racking our brains about how to bring young Giselle to us when Mr. Bunney comes back. Do you think a formal invitation would do?"

Cassie shook her head. "No, absolutely not! Mr. Duggan would rather cut off his right leg than have his daughter pay us a visit."

Hazel sighed in disappointment. "Yes, I believe you're right. We'll have to contrive a plan where they have a chance meeting."

"Hazel, I don't want to see you getting in trouble with Mr. Duggan. You have no obligation to help Mr. Bunney."

"I know that, Cassie! But in the name of love I'm

willing to nurse things along. You know how tender-hearted I am."

Cassie wanted to agree with that, but part of her knew tenderheartedness wasn't all that drove Hazel. Incurable meddlesomeness did. Bless her heart, but the old lady had had precious little romance in her own life.

"You are to be commended for your concern, Hazel," she replied. "However, you know Mr. Duggan has a legendary hot temper and does not hesitate to use violence to protect his turf."

Hazel bristled. "What? He would shoot a defenseless old lady?"

"If you trespass on his property, there's no telling what he would do." Cassie closed the journal and stood. "You have to assure me you're not about to do something foolish, Hazel."

Hazel took on a mutinous expression. "I suppose . . . but it's the outside of enough to think Mr. Duggan would be that inconsiderate."

Cassie didn't reply, only gave her boarder a stern look.

As twilight arrived the next day, she went outside to study her handiwork in the garden. It looked good, all the vegetables flourishing and spreading in all directions. The weeds had been tamed for the time being, and the shrubs had been trimmed to perfection, thanks to Ned and his nephews.

She walked to her favorite spot, the bench by the rose arbor, and sat down. She never tired of the view of the ever-changing water of the Channel and the clouds that endlessly chased each other in a variety of colors and formations. Tonight the fluffy white billows were tinged with pink and gold as the sun went below the horizon.

The sea moved restlessly, echoing the feelings in her heart. Was Dylan even now getting ready for a night of gambling, or—she pushed away the thought, but it kept creeping back, making every moment uncomfortable.

She found it difficult to enjoy the positive changes around Fairweather as she wondered if some London gentleman would be made poverty stricken just so Fairweather's roof could be rebuilt. There were no good answers to that dilemma, she thought, and the guilt would ride Dylan, not her. Not that *he* would suffer from any guilt.

She sat until darkness had fallen. The night felt balmy, the light breeze a caress on her skin. It made her uncomfortable to find how much time she spent thinking about Dylan Wenthaven and remembering the explosive quality of his mouth on hers.

It just wouldn't do.

Tired, she stretched her aching back and leaned back against the old cushion on the seat. She closed her eyes and inhaled deeply the fresh, tangy air from the sea. Within seconds she started to drift, her head tilting toward her chest.

The next thing she knew, she awakened with a tremendous pain in her neck as she gently straightened her head. "Oooh," she moaned and massaged the tender muscles. It was time to go to bed, not sit here and torture herself.

She got up and massaged her lower back, then stretched her arms over her head. Just as she started to move out of the arbor, she heard a noise at the back of the house.

Footsteps, stealthy through the grass, moved

nearby, and she could see the faint outline of a person as the moon rose over the water.

Fear chilled her blood, but she didn't cry out. Standing perfectly still, she waited to see what would happen next.

The person kept moving, right by her and through the vegetable garden. Her heart leaped into her throat as she wondered who could be sneaking around in the dark. Clearly whoever it was had no intention of making his presence known.

On shaky legs, she followed the figure. As the moon threw an ever-brighter light, she saw it was a man dressed all in black.

He looked in through the windows in the dining room and the kitchen. Evidently finding no one, he tried the back door, which wasn't locked. It usually wasn't locked at night. From now on it would be, she thought.

The only way to discover what the man wanted was to let him have entrance to the house. She would follow him at a safe distance. She remembered the previous tenants had complained of strange goings-on at night.

The house had never stood vacant, or she suspected vagrants would've taken over the property.

The kitchen door creaked as he opened it cautiously and stepped inside. She followed, her fear so strong she could barely move. What if he was waiting for her in the kitchen?

She glanced around the room, finding no one, and took the heavy iron poker, figuring it might give her some protection in the case of direct confrontation.

Walking as silently as she could, she followed the intruder into the dark hallway, where only one candle burned on a table at the bottom of the stairs. She saw him open the door to the library and step inside. He didn't close the door behind him completely, probably to prevent noise.

She tiptoed across the wooden floor, praying it wouldn't creak, knowing it usually did if you stepped on certain weak spots.

Hiding behind the door frame to the library, she peeked inside and saw he'd lighted a candle on the desk. To her surprise, he wasn't going through the papers. Instead he inspected the walls, just as she had done in the past. She didn't recognize the fellow. He looked rather young and had very dark hair and intense eyes. Possibly he was foreign.

He looked more refined than dangerous, but *why* was he inspecting the walls? She suspected he was searching for the cracks that would reveal a hiding place. Could it be he was hunting for the alleged treasure?

She could enter and confront him, but he had superior strength, and she didn't doubt for a moment he would use it.

"What's going on?" someone whispered in her ear, and she almost fainted with fright.

In the weak light from the candle on the desk, she immediately recognized Mr. Ripple, despite the ridiculous red-and-gold brocaded nightcap pressed low over his ears. She noticed vaguely that he wore a majestic dressing gown of the same material.

With a trembling finger, she pointed at the intruder. "He's searching for something. I've never seen him before."

Ripple squinted into the study, tensed, and with a mighty howl rushed into the room, his fists knotted. Cassie couldn't believe her eyes, and stiffened in fear as the men locked in combat.

THE GHOST AND MRS. WENTHAVEN   119

Ripple had the disadvantage in height, but a lot of courage. A swift battle ensued, and Ripple bombarded the villain with a series of blows that would've floored a weaker man. The stranger responded halfheartedly and ducked the last volley.

He rushed across the room, right by Cassie, who was too surprised to react.

She heard him running back the way he'd come. Ripple followed, and she kept up the rear. As they sprinted out the back door, she realized the intruder had managed to slip away in the darkness.

Ripple leaned against the wall and breathed heavily. "I . . . almost got . . . that . . . blasted scoundrel . . . excuse my . . . language."

Cassie peered into the darkness, her heart still pounding. She had never been so afraid. "You're very brave, Ripple." Her legs were shaking so badly she could barely remain standing.

"Thieves and ruffians!" Ripple spat. "I thought we would be safe in a quiet place like this."

"Yes . . . but this is no ordinary thief. I believe he is looking for a specific thing." *The same thing as I,* she thought. "Miss Elderberry saw someone skulking in the garden one morning, so it may not be the first time strangers have been on the property without our permission."

"Mark my words, Mrs. Wenthaven, the man will return. Whatever he was looking for he didn't find, and certainly there isn't anything worth stealing in the house, if you don't mind my saying so."

"You're right on that score, Ripple."

Silence hung for a moment, but Cassie didn't explain about the diary and the secret hiding places.

Ripple wiped his forehead and stared into the night. His nightcap hung askew and he righted it, obviously embarrassed by his disarray. He tied the sash of his robe prudently, his face flaming red in the light of the candle Cassie held.

"I'm sorry," he said, and crossed his arms over his chest as if shielding something that wasn't already covered by the voluminous robe.

"Without you, I don't know what I would've done."

He eyed the candlestick that she'd picked up in the hallway, and the poker. "I hope you weren't planning on defending yourself with that."

"When you're faced with a crisis, you don't think very clearly," she replied and went back into the house. "I'll have to report the incident to the constable tomorrow."

"Madam," Ripple said, following her into the kitchen. "I don't know if you're interested, but I feel the ghost has been very restless these last few days."

Cassie stiffened. "Can you express yourself a little more clearly?"

"There's an agitation in the air, as if the ghost is telling us that time is important."

Cassie didn't quite know how to respond. "If you listened to yourself, you'd find your words very strange, Ripple."

"Yes . . . be that as it may, I know, however, that the ghost wants to impart something."

Cassie remembered the diary and how she'd mysteriously found it on the floor where it had fallen from its secret hiding place. She also recalled the strangeness of the night, as if someone had been watching her. "Very well, Ripple. I will accept there might be a ghost in the house, and that he's on a mission."

"He? So you believe the stories about Captain Brooks?"

Cassie nodded. "I've read about his life and I find he was an opportunist and quite ruthless. People lost their lives at his hand, and he didn't seem to have a conscience about that."

"Life was not valued much on the high seas, Mrs. Wenthaven. It was a hard life, and still is. To survive you had to be strong. Captain Brooks is worried because things are taking too much time."

"Too much time? He's been dead for one hundred and fifty years."

"Yes, but his adversary is becoming desperate."

"What do you know about an adversary?"

"Captain Brooks did something severe to someone who didn't deserve such treatment. Until that score has been settled, he won't be able to rest."

"Yes . . . I understand." Cassie realized she had to finish reading the diary to get more clues—*if* the event or situation was mentioned. "There's no reason to put fear into the other occupants tonight. I'll tell them tomorrow."

Ripple agreed. They made sure all the doors and windows were locked downstairs. Then she thanked Ripple again and went to her room. Too torn up about the intruder to sleep, she sat down on her bed with the pillows propped up against the oak headboard and started reading the journal again.

The night was old as she finished, and she thought she had the answer she was looking for. "At least I know why Mr. Duggan upholds the feud. I might, too, if someone had destroyed my ship and stolen my goods."

Captain Brooks and his pirates had lured away the crew of the Duggan ship while it lay at anchor in the bay ready to be unloaded after a trip to the Mediterranean, then had looted and burned the vessel. With that, the Duggans had lost their livelihood and any hope of recovering their fortune. No wonder Captain Brooks couldn't find peace.

Nine

Dylan and Mr. Bunney returned to upheaval at Fairweather the next day. The constable had arrived before them and was questioning the occupants about what seemed a mixture of enquiries about the baby and some man who had entered the house unbidden on the previous night.

The Elderberry twins and Mrs. Granger were interrupting each other constantly with conflicting information.

Dylan entered the kitchen, where everyone was assembled, and his eyes sought Cassie, who sat on a chair rocking the baby in her arms. His heart squeezed with emotion, and he found it hard to breathe. She looked lovely in a simple lavender gown, her cheeks flushed and her eyes sparkling with—anger? Why would she be angry?

"What is going on here?" he asked and leaned against the door frame, ready to jump in and defend her if need be. Not that she would ever ask him to.

The conversation quieted down, and all eyes fastened on him and Mr. Bunney. Cassie gave him a long look, and again his breath caught at the intensity of their silent exchange. He realized it mattered very much to him how she would welcome him.

"Mr. Wenthaven," Constable Sweeney said pompously. He rose from the chair where he'd been sitting and adjusted his coat over his enormous paunch. "It seems there has been considerable excitement going on around here while you were gone." He proceeded to tell about the intruder and how he'd gotten away despite Ripple's valiant pursuit.

Ripple looked important and dapper as always, almost more dashing than his employer. But he lowered his eyes to the floor as Dylan glanced at him.

"Ripple, it appears I owe you immense gratitude for taking care of my house in my absence," Dylan said.

Sweeney said, "We're speculating that the man might be connected to the wee orphan in some way, but Mrs. Wenthaven opposes that idea."

Dylan looked at Cassie, wanting so much to talk to her in private. He beckoned to her even as Mr. Bunney requested Ripple's assistance. She didn't look too eager to comply, but she hoisted the baby into her arms and went with Dylan into the library.

He closed the door behind them and pulled out a chair for her, but she chose to sit in one of the worn wing chairs by the window.

"I'm sorry I wasn't here to protect you," he said.

"Ripple and I did quite well on our own, but we never discovered the identity of the intruder. We had never seen him before. I believe he's not a local person, but rather someone hired for the job."

"The job?"

The baby gurgled and smiled toothlessly. It was definitely a Wenthaven smile, Dylan thought, disturbed. He pushed away the thought and concentrated on Cassie and the business at hand.

"I found Captain Brooks's personal diary, and I've

spent the last few days—and nights—reading it. It looks as if he perpetrated a great crime against Duggan's ancestor, thereby creating the feud that still rages."

With patience he milked the whole story from her.

"I believe Captain Brooks will haunt this estate until the injustice has been rectified," she said.

He smiled. "You never believed in the old ghost story, did you?"

She shook her head. "No, but several people have actually seen the captain, and I certainly felt his presence the other night. Besides, he gave me the journal."

"This is getting more intriguing by the minute."

She told him about how she'd found the journal on the floor of her armoire. "Captain Brooks hid the loot he stole from the Duggan ancestor somewhere on this estate, and somehow Mr. Duggan knows about it and is looking for it. I'm surprised no one has found it so far."

"So you plan to find it first?" he asked, feeling a strong desire to catch her and kiss her sweet lips until she went limp in his arms. Of course, he didn't do any of it. Why he was drawn to her was a mystery to him.

The love Mr. Bunney was talking about he'd never experienced, but looking into Cassie's eyes did something to him. If he'd been of poetic nature he might've written a verse to her expressive brown eyes.

Not that he would, though. He certainly didn't have a poetic bone in his body. Her eyes did have a velvet sense to them, but that's as far as his flights of fancy went.

"If the treasure exists, of course I want to find it

first!" she said. "There may be something we can sell and make a profit to apply toward the repairs."

He debated silently with himself as he worried about her response, then said, "We won't have a problem repairing the roof. I won a large sum of money the other night at the card tables at Watier's."

A cloud came over her face, the light in her eyes dimmed, and he read disappointment in the droop of her lips. "Oh."

"There's no reason for you to make a comment on how I choose to pay for the repairs," he said curtly.

"I hardly call that a 'comment,' " she said defensively.

"But your face speaks volumes," he replied. "And spare me the lectures."

She stood, anger flaming in her face. "I had no intention of lecturing you, but it's clear your conscience already has."

"Conscience? That's the outside of enough! There's no reason why my conscience would be involved in this. It never has been and never will be."

She didn't say anything, and the baby started a piercing cry that wore on his already raw nerves. She bounced the boy on her shoulder. "There, there, I know you're upset," she crooned softly. "Mrs. Granger might have some warm milk for you."

Without another look, she walked toward the door.

"You're just going to leave without arguing your point, Cassie?"

"I argued enough with James, and he paid absolutely no attention to anything I said, so I avoid battles I can't win. If you choose to fleece other people who probably fleeced someone else, possibly someone who is an innocent to the ways of gambling, it's your choice. Robbing innocents is not something I would choose as a source of livelihood."

"You're clutching at straws, Cassie. Just because James had no scruples doesn't mean I'm cut from the same cloth. I choose my opponents carefully, and I would never fleece a greenhorn. Your bitterness toward James is understandable, but it has nothing to do with me."

"There our conversation ends," she said. "I don't know if you're as selfish as James was, but you went to the same schools and were raised by the same people. I can't see there would be much difference."

"Generalizations, Cassie. I'd appreciate it if you don't judge me until you know me better."

Silence simmered between them as she stood by the door. He read the mutiny on her face.

"Did you make any progress on the shrubs? I noticed the front of the house looks very tidy compared to when we left," he said.

"Ned and his nephews worked hard." Her breasts heaved as she took a deep breath. "But I've made up my mind after listening to your account. I hereby resign my position as your steward. I can't ally myself with a situation that is not of highest moral standard."

"Moral standard? Who are you to judge?" Anger boiled in his chest. "You're very high in the instep, Cassie."

"But at least I know what I believe in."

He couldn't say anything to that. Why her beliefs mattered to him was incomprehensible.

"I shall remove myself shortly, just as soon as I can connect with my father's friends in the north country. I heard some time ago their daughter might need a governess. I may be leaving if I can gain that position."

"There's no reason for you to leave," he said tiredly. "You're welcome to stay for as long as you like. That's the least I can do for my sister-in-law."

"I'm not a charity project," she said and marched out the door.

"Stubborn woman," he said to himself and felt like kicking something.

He returned to the kitchen. Cassie sat stiff-backed on a chair, cradling the baby.

Constable Sweeney said investigations were under way as to the identity of the baby, but everyone locally believed some impoverished servant had left the infant on the back step, never to return again.

"We're willing to take him over to the poorhouse," the constable said to Dylan.

"I don't see why he should have to suffer such a fate," Dylan said. "I know it has added to Mrs. Granger's burden to look after him, but I doubt it's sound to release him into your care until we know more." Dylan slanted a glance at Cassie and noted the faint expression of approval on her face.

At least he'd said something right.

"Then there's the mystery of the baby's rattle, which you concluded comes from the Wenthaven family."

"Yes . . . it's a mystery how that ended up in the boy's basket, but someone must've stolen it from Lord Seffington's coffers. He was the last of the old generation."

"So all the heirlooms have gone to you, Mr. Wenthaven?"

Dylan shook his head. "No, everything except Fairweather went to the other branch of the family.

My cousins' children. There were lots of heirlooms, and I don't know who got what. Possibly the rattle was lost as Seffington House got cleared out."

"London is far from Fairweather, especially for a servant on foot," Cassie commented. "And how would they know where to find Fairweather?"

"That's a mystery only the mother of the child can solve for us," Sweeney said. "I won't leave any stone unturned. 'Tis highly irresponsible to leave one's child into the care of strangers."

No one could argue that point.

"I think we have all grown quite fond of the mite," Mrs. Granger said. "He has a sunny disposition, he does. No trouble 'tall."

" 'Tis good for Fairweather to 'ave little tykes 'ere," Ned Biggins said from his stool by the hearth. "Precious long ago we 'eard the patter of tiny feet." He glanced apologetically at Dylan.

"I'm not *that* old," Dylan said with a laugh.

" 'Twas long enough ago, and a 'andful ye were, you and yer twin brother. Always into mischief."

Dylan slanted a glance at Cassie and could almost read the accusing thought in her mind: "Still into it." He found he had no regrets for his past. He had lived with honor, even if he fell short in some people's eyes. A weight fell off his chest as he remembered the truth: He had always lived with principle.

Something, a sense of new life, rose within him like sap in a tree in spring. Because he had a quick mind and a deft hand, he could now start to rebuild his past. He looked around the kitchen, with its ancient hearth, its sagging porch, and its worn cupboards. The hands that had once built this place had experienced pride and accomplishment. So could he.

"The child has a home here until we can find his

parents and sort something out," he said with authority. "Just as the rest of you have a home as long as you need it." He gave Cassie another glance, but she quickly looked away, her cheeks reddening.

Feeling light, he turned toward the door. "I need a breath of fresh air."

Cassie watched him leave, her insides turning over with uncomfortable feelings. Had she been too harsh in her judgment of him? She knew she had, but how could she ever admit such a thing? He hadn't looked overly perturbed, and his step had had a decided spring in it as he walked outside. As with geese, water—or criticism—seemed to run right off him.

She couldn't remember a time when she'd felt in the clutches of such turmoil, and so *humiliated* for some reason. To live in poverty held no dignity, and having so few choices brought more frustration than she could bear.

Mrs. Granger must have felt her tumultuous emotions and came to relieve her of the baby. "There, dearie, be a good boy now." The cook hoisted the boy into her plump arms, then settled him in the crook of her elbow. Children and grandchildren had rested in that same spot, and they must have thrived. Rarely had she met such a loving and patient woman as Mrs. Granger, Cassie thought.

Feeling restless, she went to her room and picked up the captain's diary. There had to be something more, something that told the exact hiding space of the treasure.

Standing by the window, she looked out to sea. The beauty of the scenery stole her breath away. The sun slanted across the ever-moving water, throwing handfuls of diamonds on the waves.

She inhaled deeply and leaned out the open window. The tattered curtain wafted across her arm, and as she moved it away, she noticed that Dylan stood on the terrace below. His hand shaded his eyes against the glare of the sunlight, and as if he'd felt her gaze, he looked up at her. The shaft of a spear or an arrow could not have pierced her more profoundly. His gaze touched the very depths of her heart, making her feel faint and incredibly alive at the same time.

Ten

"I'm fading away like last autumn's roses," Mr. Bunney complained a week later. "If I don't get a glimpse of my Beloved, I shall completely wither away."

Cassie noticed his pinched look and felt sorry for him. "You look like you don't sleep well at night."

He gave her a wounded, outraged look. "How can I when I'm tormented with thoughts about her every hour, every minute of the day? It's a sickness, my dear. I'm in the throes of the most terribly agony."

"Oh, poor, poor boy," Hazel crooned, and Hermione chimed in. Hazel gave Mr. Bunney a shrewd glance, then threaded her embroidery needle, the tip of her tongue firmly lodged between her front teeth as she concentrated on the eye of the needle. "You can always help us sort our tangled embroidery silks to distract your thoughts. It takes a mathematical talent like yours to figure out the knots."

Hazel is spreading it on rather thick, Cassie thought with a rueful grin. Mr. Bunney soaked up the compliments like a daisy soaks up the rain.

"I'm delighted you can see some of my strengths," he said importantly. "Now, if Giselle could see any of my talents, she would do everything in her power to reach my side."

"Poor Mr. Bunney. But you must remember she's guarded by that madman Mr. Duggan and her dragon of a chaperone," Hazel said. "Miss Giselle does not take a step without them knowing about it."

"Blast and damn!" Mr. Bunney's eyes grew huge and he turned crimson with embarrassment. "I'm so sorry; my emotions ran away with me, but there's no excuse for my language."

"Didn't your mother wash out your mouth with carbolic soap?" Hazel asked severely.

Mr. Bunney looked confused, and Cassie knew he had no clue what carbolic soap was.

"All I want is a *glimpse*," Mr. Bunney continued. "It would be engraved forever on my mind."

Cassie bent over the journal in her lap and bit down on her bottom lip to stop herself from laughing. Poor Mr. Bunney. But she had an inkling of what he was feeling. A few weeks ago it would have been an alien world, but today, she experienced some of that agony he was describing, only because of one fiery look from Dylan's bright blue-green eyes.

"Well, as a matter of fact," Hazel said, "I believe Miss Giselle takes the air at the same time every day. At eleven she goes out on one of those spavined horses Mr. Duggan keeps in his stables."

"*Spavined?* You must be about in your head, Hazel," Cassie said. "His horses are all thoroughbreds."

"Be that as it may, I just don't care for his cattle. They are forever galloping hither and yon, kicking up dust and leaving their prints on everything. Every path around here is treacherous with horseshoe indentations."

"Well, if you're not steady on your pins, I can

understand your concern," Mr. Bunney said. " 'Tis thoughtless of your neighbor to cause such inconvenience for you."

"They have to run somewhere," Cassie defended the poor horses.

"And so do we," Hazel said, bristling.

"Dear, we don't run, do we?" Hermione pointed out timidly. She hastily averted her gaze after having spoken so boldly.

"Be quiet, Hermione," Hazel boomed. "I walk at a rather brisk clip, and I'm proud of it."

Cassie sensed the conversation was about to go completely overboard. "If there wasn't that stupid family feud, we could invite Giselle and her chaperone to Fairweather, but they dislike us more than they do the worst criminal."

Mr. Bunney got up and paced the room. His arm was still in a sling, but Cassie could find no fault with his immaculate coat of blue superfine, his snug pale yellow pantaloons, and his elegant cravat.

Ripple had really outdone himself this morning, as if Mr. Bunney would descend on Bond Street at any minute, instead of rusticating in the country where no one cared about cravats tied into a Waterfall, the cut of a coat, or the shine of topboots. Mr. Bunney swore by a mixture of champagne and blacking to polish up his Hessian boots to a mirror-like shine.

"There has to be *something* we can do to reach Giselle," Mr. Bunney said in high agitation. "We are a group of great minds, so between us we ought to be able to come up with a plan. I won't be able to withstand this pressure for another moment."

Cassie said, "Other than to kidnap her, I don't know—"

Mr. Bunney brightened. "You may have hit upon

the brightest solution, dear Cassie! If we bring her here for tea one afternoon, her dragon might not be the wiser. Besides, dragons always have to take their afternoon nap."

Cassie could see his mind working, and she had a premonition that she would regret ever mentioning the word kidnapping. She feared Mr. Bunney was capable of almost any kind of desperate measure to see the object of his affection.

If she'd known Giselle better, she might've been of some assistance, but she couldn't think of anything that would solve the dilemma.

"I doubt, Mr. Bunney, that Giselle would take a favorable view of being kidnapped," Cassie said to dampen his enthusiasm. "She might be violently set against it."

"If she has the slightest tender spot in her heart for me, which I believe she does, she won't mind. 'Twill be an adventure, don't you see?" Mr. Bunney's eyes lit up with a fire nothing would quench, and Cassie thought he was quite fond of adventures, especially of the romantic kind.

She worried for a moment over the consequences of such adventures, but realized she wasn't involved, and never would be.

However, Fate conspired to give Mr. Bunney an opportunity to express his love, and the event had no real tinge of adventure about it. Later that day a note arrived addressed to Mr. Dylan Wenthaven from the Dowager Lady Pender with an invitation for an *al fresco* tea party at nearby Pender Hall. She wrote that she had recently returned from her London life and wanted some familiar faces around her as she got back into the social circle of her neighbors.

Pender Hall had never been the Earl of Pender's

main residence, but she liked its location so close to the sea.

"We're all invited," Dylan said as he scanned the note. "I suppose we'll have to polish the mud off our boots and darn the holes in our clothes."

"Ohhh," Hazel said and clapped her hand to her mouth. "We're going to a society gathering—after all these *years.*"

"Yes, you'll have to make sure your finest dresses are aired. Lady Pender is a lady of great dignity, but she also has a great sense of humor," Dylan said.

"She needed that, living with that stick-in-the-mud Pender for all those years. A sourpuss of the first degree he was," Mr. Bunney said. "She blossomed after he passed away five years ago, and was quite a popular hostess in London."

"When is it?" Cassie asked, intrigued, but worrying she wouldn't have anything decent to wear.

"It's next Saturday at four o'clock," Dylan replied and sent the invitation around the table.

Cassie spent the next few days going over her wardrobe. She finally decided on a gray empire dress with short sleeves and a charcoal overskirt embroidered with black vines. It had seen its better days, but at least it hadn't been mended like so many of her other gowns. Due to its somber color, she hadn't worn it much, since there had been no entertaining during her time of mourning.

It took her almost three hours to get ready, what with coaxing her flyaway hair into a becoming arrangement with orderly curls around her face, and a tiny lace cap attached on top of her head. She didn't like caps, but as a widow she had to wear one while in society, or be frowned upon. If she followed the rules correctly, she should still be wearing black entirely, but she couldn't stand it.

Ned Biggins had polished up the old barouche and borrowed some decent horses from the local hostelry. It would be a rare treat to go out in style, Cassie thought.

The Elderberry twins twittered with excitement, Hazel in a deep purple gown, and Hermione in plum-hued satin. Their dresses were sadly out of style, but they didn't seem to mind. They fluttered fans and constantly adjusted their gray buns, which held an amazing assortment of artificial birds and fruit.

The men looked worldly in fine coats and breeches, all in the latest styles as dictated by that arbiter of fashion in London, Beau Brummell.

Mr. Bunney had adopted a subtly mournful look, and with his arm in the black silk sling, he exuded an air of needing tender nurturing.

"You look lovely," Dylan said to Cassie.

Her cheeks grew hot, and she wanted to say he looked handsome and virile, but no words came to her lips. She nodded curtly. "Thank you." She had been avoiding him for days, but now she could not run away.

"Gray actually becomes you," he added. "It really brings out the roses in your cheeks." His eyes twinkled with mischief, and to her chagrin, her face grew hotter.

"You're very observant," she said, a hitch in her voice.

"When it comes to you, I am," he murmured so only she could hear him.

Her heartbeat escalated, and her knees weakened most alarmingly. His words had a more profound effect on her than she liked.

He addressed the group. "Are we all ready?" He helped the ladies into the barouche, which creaked with every movement. The cracked leather seats snagged fabric, but everyone kept their dismay to themselves.

"One of these days we shall have a new carriage and a pair of fine bays to pull it," Dylan said as he closed the door and sat down on the opposite side of the ladies, Mr. Bunney next to him.

Surrounded by an immaculate park, Pender Hall was a sprawling sandstone building that had been added to over the centuries. The front entrance held the simple elegance of the seventeenth century, with windows of leaded diamond-shaped panes and a beautifully carved door that appeared impossible to move. But move it did, on well-oiled hinges.

The butler showed them out to the vast terrace in the back, where an ample tea table had been set up. A group of violinists played Handel music on a dais partly shrouded with towering plants. The view of the Channel was just as breathtaking as the one at Fairweather.

"*There* you are," a tiny gray-haired woman cried out. The Dowager Lady Pender held out both of her hands to Dylan, who bent down and kissed her cheek.

"As lovely as ever, Elisa."

"You young rapscallion." The dowager slapped him playfully with her fan. "Haven't changed a bit, even if there's some sadness in your eyes. Your difficulties have matured you."

Cassie noticed he became uncomfortable, and knew instinctively he still keenly felt the loss of his twin.

"You haven't changed at all, Elisa. You're as observant as you always were." He took a breath. "And as confrontational as ever, but that goes without saying."

Cassie agreed that the dowager looked elegant in a fashionable lavender silk gown with a lace overdress and pearls around her neck and in her ears. Her hair had been coaxed into the latest style of short curls topped with a lace-edged cap.

"And who is this?" the dowager asked as she turned toward Cassie.

Dylan introduced everyone to the hostess. The dowager turned to Cassie and said, "I knew your late husband."

Cassie expected to hear something positive added on, but was not surprised when the lady didn't elaborate. Not many people had liked James, and he hadn't liked a great many people. Cassie had never quite understood where his condescending outlook on life came from.

"Now that I know you live at Fairweather, I'll have the opportunity to visit and have some lovely chats," the dowager continued. She winked at Dylan. "Conversations with gentlemen are never the same."

"We are a dull lot, aren't we?" Dylan drawled.

"Speak for yourself," Mr. Bunney said in wounded tones.

Commotion at the door drew everyone's attention. Cassie heard a suppressed groan from Mr. Bunney and realized the arriving guests were Miss Duggan and her chaperone Lady Cutting, Duggan's sister. Oh dear, what would evolve from this encounter? At least Mr. Duggan was not included in the party.

Mr. Bunney emitted another groan and his face turned quite pale.

"Miss Duggan and Lady Cutting, how very kind of you to accept my invitation," the dowager said.

"Just as mine was, your sojourn in London was cut short after the young lady twisted her ankle, but you look quite recovered, Giselle. Then there was the loss in your family also."

Giselle's name suited her perfectly, Cassie thought. She had a doelike quality, her limbs slender and graceful and her eyes warm and expressive. It didn't surprise Cassie that Mr. Bunney had developed such an infatuation for the lady.

Giselle's eyelids flickered in alarm as she laid eyes on Mr. Bunney, but she held her composure admirably.

Still pale, he took her hand into his visibly trembling one and kissed it. Lady Cutting pulled Giselle away immediately and Cassie suspected she wanted to leave, but that would be excessively rude.

The frail tunes of the violins wove across the terrace, and the dowager invited everyone to sit down. The Elderberry twins soon held her attention. Cassie tried to start a conversation with Lady Cutting, but the lady had nothing but rebuffs.

"I realize you're privy to the feud between our families," Cassie said at last, "but let me assure you that I have nothing personally against any one of you. I would prefer to see the feud put to rest."

She was interested to see if Lady Cutting would acknowledge the feud.

"My brother, Mr. Duggan, is adamant about keeping the feud alive," Lady Cutting said, "and that's his choice." She looked uncomfortable. "I have nothing to do with it; I'm only here to watch over Giselle until she's safely married." She threw an uneasy glance at Mr. Bunney. "I'm sure Julius would be enraged to find out that Mr. Bunney, who was responsible for Giselle's sprained ankle, is one of the guests here."

Mr. Bunney took his gaze from Giselle across the table for one moment. "I'll have you know if it hadn't been for me, she might have broken her leg." His voice trembled with emotion. "I want nothing but the best for Miss Duggan, and that should be very obvious, if you'd care to notice it."

Lady Cutting put her nose in the air. "Mr. Bunney, you're a *predator* in the worst sense, and I'll do anything in my power to keep Giselle safe from the likes of you, or I might have to taste Mr. Duggan's wrath."

Cassie glanced at Giselle, who looked uncomfortable. A wave of red suffused Mr. Bunney's face, but he held his temper in check admirably. Silence hung heavy over the table.

"I shall just content myself knowing that I'm in Miss Duggan's presence. In no manner would I push myself on her against her wishes."

Cassie thought he would choke on the last words. It must've taken all he had to be so humble. True to his word, he gazed in a misty way across the table, and an iron statue would've melted under so much tenderness. Giselle shifted in her seat, two red spots glowing in her cheeks.

What would've been a simple tea party became a morass of unspoken emotions. Cassie felt quite exhausted as a plate of glazed cakes was put in front of her. A footman served scones and clotted cream, and another carried a fragrant spice cake around the table. A third served tea from a silver pot into fragile porcelain cups, treating everyone like royalty. Cassie enjoyed the ceremony.

Dylan sat across from her and must've seen that she particularly liked the iced currant cakes. He pushed his toward her, and she debated if she should accept it. His gaze urged her, and with a shrug, she took it. He chuckled.

"A very small victory, but it counts," he said quietly. He glanced at Lady Cutting on the other side of Cassie and added under his breath, "I don't know why it is that ladies are so hard to please."

"Mayhap we don't want to be indebted to 'predators,' " Cassie said in a joking tone of voice.

"By Jupiter, you would think the entire male species is nothing but vile and calculating. We're quite capable of benevolent and supportive actions—most of the time."

"I'm sorry if I sound bitter, but I've learned to rely solely on myself."

"As I see it, you're a giving person, but you don't know how to accept gifts given to you, not even the smallest thing like a cake, without debating over it."

"It depends who the giver is," she said. The tension around her made her on edge. She had no desire to start an argument with Dylan, but that seemed to be the only way they could communicate.

He didn't take the bait. "You have precious little experience in that department. I'd think you're intelligent enough to trust those who show obvious caring qualities."

"You include yourself in that category?" She nibbled on her cake but couldn't taste a thing.

His long fingers played with a silver teaspoon. "Of course I do. I trust my instincts, and when I trust someone, I give wholeheartedly."

He was in so many words telling her he trusted her. That knowledge wrapped around her heart like cotton. "Your instincts may be correct, but I daresay it's wrong to barge in where one is not invited."

"Who said anything about barging? I look before I walk, as any *predator* would," he teased. "Caution is in my blood."

He was right. She couldn't picture him barging anywhere, or stepping on someone's toes because of carelessness.

He continued, "If I'd met you before James did, you wouldn't be so bitter against gentlemen now. He always was the type to barge over people's emotions."

Oh, how right he was, but she had no desire to start any tirades against James. "That part of my life is long gone. I find I have peace and I don't need very much to be happy. I certainly don't need conflict of any kind, but I have to say I encounter it everywhere around me. Just look at poor Mr. Bunney. Rarely do you see such suffering."

"He has a severe case of Cupid's arrow, and until you have been pierced by it, you don't know what it's like."

"Do you, Dylan?"

He hesitated, avoiding her eyes for a second. "When I was eighteen, I suffered greatly from that cruel angel's arrow. Her name was Lucy, and she is the daughter of one of Seffington's friends. As far as I know she's now happily wed with children, so that suffering meant nothing. Temporary insanity, I call it. But if it's reciprocated, Heaven and Earth can be moved by the force of that love shared. Don't you think so?"

"It rarely is returned, though. Am I wrong? That's why the emotions are so strong. The sufferer imagines what could be, and in the imagination everything is perfect, of course."

"Yes . . . I fear there's some truth to that, Cassie, but I suspect I'm a lot more idealistic than you are.

Full of noble feelings and hopes. Perhaps that's childish of me."

Cassie didn't think so. She could use some more noble feelings herself and not always be so rational. "Father always told me not to build dream castles, as they were unrealistic and always disappointed you in the end."

"Without dream castles there's no color, really no hope of something better," he said, toying with a spoon.

Cassie felt nervous treading boggy territory. She had no desire to explore her emotions in Dylan's company, especially since she didn't know what to tell him. His presence stirred up emotions she didn't know she had, *unsafe* emotions in her opinion.

"You're speechless," he continued.

"How can I argue with hope?" she asked. "It's one of mankind's only redeeming qualities, to believe that there's something better to strive for."

"Then you do agree? About dream castles?"

"If you equate those with hope, I suppose I have to," she replied reluctantly. "I don't know how we got into this discussion. There seems to be a logical flaw somewhere."

"We're not talking about mathematics, Cassie, though I suspect you have an excellent sense for numbers. As you have an excellent sense for everything else. There has to be an imperfection somewhere in your character, but I've not been able to find it."

"Everyone has their gifts." She laughed. "This is a ridiculous conversation."

"Circumstances sometimes call for the ridiculous to dispel the tension."

"Tension? What—" Her heart pounded, and she felt slightly dizzy.

"You know very well what I'm talking about, Cassie. You can't pretend you don't feel it. Every time we're in the same room, we could cut the air with a knife."

"That's because we don't get along," she replied as heat rose in her cheeks.

He gave her a long, probing look. "That's only your viewpoint. I might have a completely different perspective."

His every word challenged her, and she cast about for the perfect answer. Nothing came to her, though she usually had no problems in that department.

She was relieved when their hostess interrupted the conversation. One more word from him, and she would've been forced to excuse herself from the table.

Eleven

"You look quite perturbed, Mrs. Wenthaven," the dowager said, fanning herself. "Is the sun bothering you? It would be very awkward for you to have a fainting spell. I could never live with myself."

Cornered like an animal, with everyone looking at her, Cassie glanced around for an escape route. From the corner of her eye, she noticed the smile playing on Dylan's lips and the glitter behind his half-closed eyelids as he leaned back in his chair. The wretch was laughing at her!

"No, the sun has never bothered me," Cassie said, "but sometimes I find the company a challenge—no offense intended. You're nothing if not gracious, and I appreciate this opportunity to meet you, Lady Pender."

"Pooh, no need to stand on formalities here." The dowager gave Dylan a shrewd look. "If that rogue has given you something to blush about, I personally shall punish him."

Dylan raised his eyebrows. "Now, Elisa, what would make you think that I would ever embarrass a lady?"

"Because you have that wicked twinkle in your

eye. I've seen it before, ever since you were in short-coats, so don't try to bamboozle me."

Dylan only lifted his shoulders in a shrug and smiled mysteriously. The dowager tut-tutted, and Cassie wished the tea party was over.

"I would *never* trust the young gentlemen these days," Lady Cutting said with a sniff. "They are forever looking for ways to take advantage of unsuspecting females."

Mr. Bunney heaved a trembling sigh that everyone could hear, and threw a glance at Giselle that bore all the pain and longing in his heart. Cassie felt sorry for him for the hundredth time and glanced at Giselle. The young woman had a dreamy look in her eye and a warm blush in her cheeks. It was clear his soulful glances had touched her. Undoubtedly Giselle was well aware of his tender feelings, and most likely returned them.

This surprised Cassie. Perhaps there was hope for Mr. Bunney's heart when all was said and done—if Mr. Duggan could be convinced of Mr. Bunney's sincerity. Cassie doubted, however, that Mr. Duggan cared a fig for Mr. Bunney's finer feelings, or Giselle's. The size of the suitor's bank account would be the deciding factor in Giselle's future. It usually was.

Mr. Bunney discreetly pushed over a small bowl with sweetmeats to Giselle, and Cassie was the only one who noticed the clandestine move as Lady Cutting kept complaining about the horrible manners of the younger generation.

Giselle lowered her gaze and timidly took one of the chocolate bonbons from the bowl. A strange feeling of loss stabbed Cassie as she watched them. No gentleman had ever given her such a melting glance of love.

For a disconcerting moment, she felt like crying. Tears pushed at the inside of her eyelids and burned in her eyes, and she looked at her hands folded in her lap.

The dowager broke into Lady Cutting's complaints. "I really don't think the younger generation is so terrible. I remember in my day how we used to fool our parents—"

"Lady Pender!" Lady Cutting slapped her hands to Giselle's ears, and the young woman jumped in her seat as if caught doing something wicked.

"Oh, pooh! Don't be a hypocrite, Lady Cutting. Don't tell me you were an angel every day of your life."

Lady Cutting bristled. "I certainly never dreamed of doing anything against my parents' wishes. My sisters and I were models of decorum—always!"

That silenced everyone at the table until the dowager waved to the footmen waiting by the terrace door.

"All of you must sample my special rum cake. The Prince Regent once offered to pay a small fortune for the recipe, but as you can understand, it's a family secret that will go to the grave with me."

An audible sigh of relief went through the guests as everyone concentrated on the masterpiece carried in on an elegant porcelain platter.

"It is as sweet and spicy as anything you'll ever taste," the dowager said with satisfaction. She made sure everyone got a large piece—except Lady Cutting, who received a decidedly stingy slice.

Laughter suddenly bubbled up in Cassie's chest. The dowager had no difficulty finding ways to show her disapproval. Lady Cutting noted the slight and pursed her lips until they resembled a prune.

Mr. Bunney couldn't eat a bite, nor could Giselle. They gazed at each other in silent wonder.

"What do you think, Cassie?" Dylan asked.

"They are in love," she said dreamily.

"About the rum cake, I mean," he chided, and threw an amused glance at his enamored friend.

"Oh . . ." Cassie had never felt so embarrassed. If she'd known the afternoon would turn into this fiasco, she never would have come. How could Dylan make fun of her? What had gotten into him—an evil spirit who wanted nothing more than to see her mortified?

"The cake is excellent, of course," she said, but could barely swallow the small piece in her mouth. "No wonder the Prince Regent wanted the recipe."

"He's quite fond of his food and drink," Dylan said, "as his wide girth will attest."

Cassie gulped down the last of her tea, wishing again that the party was over.

"I'm so happy to be back in this bucolic idyll," the dowager said. "The competition and the extravagance of the gentry is tedious, to say the least. I got excessively bored with the whole Season."

"But just imagine all the influential people you can meet," Lady Cutting said, her face set in lines of disapproval. "And the powerful connections you can make for the future."

The dowager's eyes narrowed as she gave Lady Cutting a penetrating look. "I find such an outlook shallow and calculating."

Clearly the dowager was quickly making an enemy, Cassie thought, but she didn't seem to care. Lady

Cutting could not afford to alienate the dowager, who had all the social influence Lady Cutting sought.

"My own influence is not insignificant," Lady Cutting said, her expression sour. "And you have to think about the next generation. They have no sense of their own—none whatsoever." She gave Giselle a look that could've withered a rose on the vine.

Perhaps Giselle wasn't as meek as she looked, Cassie thought. Could she possibly have any opinions of her own while having Lady Cutting as a shepherd? Sometimes the most docile young ladies hid a deeply stubborn streak.

Finally the dowager ate the last of her rum cake and patted her mouth with a flawless napkin. A footman helped to pull out her chair. "Let's take a stroll in the garden," she said. "The gentlemen can carry our parasols."

Mr. Bunney leaped to his feet as if already looking for Giselle's umbrella, but Cassie knew it would be a lost cause before it happened.

Lady Cutting hustled the young lady away from the gentlemen and put her considerable bulk between them. Every line of her body exuded disapproval. Mr. Bunney's face took on a hangdog expression.

"Buck up, old friend," Dylan said and slapped Mr. Bunney's shoulder.

Mr. Bunney flinched, and nursed his arm as if Dylan had hit too close to the wound. "So near yet so far away," he said. "She's an unreachable star in the celestial canopy. I can only gaze and yearn for her."

"Don't be a sapskull, Eddie. She's right here. Much more than we could've hoped for." Dylan fell into step with Cassie. "Would you be interested in aiding true love on its course?"

"You mean contrivance and subterfuge?"

Dylan raised his eyebrows and gave her a level look. "If you want to put it in those terms, then yes. Let's contrive something for my friend and the object of his heart."

They followed the dowager and the others down the path. Mr. Bunney tried to sidle up to Giselle, but found himself barred at every corner. Lady Cutting took chaperoning seriously.

Cassie debated the proposition, but, yes, she wanted to help Mr. Bunney. She'd grown rather fond of the silly man, even if he annoyed her at times. "Very well. What do you propose?"

Dylan's face split in a wide grin. "I knew you had a streak of adventure buried deep down, Cassie. It's been long in coming out."

"I assure you, it's still deeply under control, so don't get too enthusiastic," she replied dryly.

"But when it blossoms, there'll be no stopping you."

"Your reasoning has many flaws, but we won't get into that now. How are we going to help Mr. Bunney?"

"The dowager has a maze that is quite ingenious. We could get Lady Cutting hopelessly lost, and Eddie and Giselle found together. Eddie won't lose any time declaring himself, and if she has any feelings for him, he'll know."

Cassie felt a spurt of excitement. "A maze! I haven't been inside one since I was a child. I enjoy getting lost and figuring my way out."

"I'm sure your logic gets quite an exercise as you calculate the turns in the hedges," he drawled, a shadow of that grin still lingering on his face.

"You just follow your nose, don't you?" she asked, and found herself smiling.

"I have developed a rather keen instinct over time," he said. "It rarely leads me wrong." He called out to the dowager and voiced the suggestion that the guests would like to experience the maze.

"Well, it's the finest one in the south counties," the dowager said. "And don't try to push through the yew hedges. You'll get hopelessly stuck and your clothing will be ruined."

"I don't know," Lady Cutting said with a frown. "I think we must return home."

"Aunt Martha!" Giselle exclaimed in her breathy voice and fluttered her hands. "Just this once. I have never been in a maze before."

"Just a lot of walking on paths that look exactly the same," Lady Cutting said, but then she must've noted the mutiny in the young woman's face and recalled that she lived in her brother's house, which would be a precarious situation at best, Cassie believed.

"Oh, very well! Just another hour then, and I'll go with you to make sure you don't get lost, Giselle."

The dowager and Dylan exchanged amused glances, and Cassie figured the hostess knew why he had requested a trip to the maze. The dowager could prove to be a great ally in this mission.

With squeals of excitement, Hazel and Hermione hurried in before everyone else. The dowager marshaled Lady Cutting and Giselle through the opening and gave Dylan a wink over her shoulder.

Cassie entered behind the women and tried to pay attention to every turn so she could get out without getting lost.

Dylan and Mr. Bunney exchanged a low-voiced conversation behind her, and she could sense Mr. Bunney's excitement. After a short time, they disappeared around a corner, and Cassie found herself alone, as the others had made a different turn ahead of her. The quest was to get to the middle first, and Cassie enjoyed the challenge.

Half an hour later, she was both hot and thirsty. The center of the maze was nowhere in sight, and her feet had started to ache. Her slippers gave her no support on the sandy lanes. Where was the center?

She made another turn, and another. In the distance she heard voices—Hazel's twittering and Lady Cutting's peevish complaints. They hadn't found the center, either. Lady Cutting was calling out Giselle's name over and over.

Cassie almost wanted to give up, but as she rounded the next corner, she bumped into Dylan.

"Had enough?" he asked, laughing. "This is the most devious maze ever planted, I think."

She had to admit defeat. "I think everyone is lost."

"Eddie and Giselle aren't. Even as we speak they are having a rendezvous."

"Where?"

"Let me show you." He took her hand, and she quelled the urge to pull away. His hand felt warm and comforting around hers. Totally comfortable, in fact.

They made two turns and he slowed down, putting a finger across his lips. Cassie's heart pounded as she glanced around the corner of the hedge. There was the center of the maze, a rose arbor with a stone bench in the middle and a sparkling fountain that tinkled over tiers of marble.

She could drink the whole thing, she thought, and saw the two people on the bench. Well, only Giselle was sitting on the bench. Mr. Bunney was on his knees at her feet.

Cassie held her breath as she watched the romantic

scene in front of her. She couldn't hear Mr. Bunney's words, but she was sure they were well chosen. Giselle sat ramrod straight and demure, but her face glowed with love, and her smile could've melted the hardest heart.

"How did you accomplish this?" Cassie whispered.

"The dowager sensed what was going on and sent Hazel and Lady Cutting down a path that will take them in circles endlessly. I know this maze, and the dowager brought Giselle. Then she went back to the house to take a nap."

Cassie suppressed a gurgle of laughter, her hand pressed to her mouth. "Lady Cutting must be beside herself."

Dylan pulled her down another path. "Let's leave them alone for a while. Eddie has a lot to say to Giselle. He's been carrying his love inside for a long time."

Cassie looked away, suddenly embarrassed.

"Not that you would know anything about that," he teased her. "Love, that is."

She squared her shoulders. "That's right. I have been spared the embarrassment of it all so far."

The sun was beating down on her parasol, and no air moved around the tall yew hedges. Perspiration dampened her skin, and she dabbed discreetly at her hairline, but knew that the moisture would curl her hair disastrously. Not that it mattered—or did it? It was only Dylan standing before her, and what he thought was unimportant.

He took her umbrella from her hand and furled it, then leaned it against the hedge. She stood, undecided about what to do next. She stared at him, mesmerized, as he turned back to her.

"What are you doing? I need my umbrella."

"In a minute. For now, it's in my way." He placed both hands on the sides of her face and looked deeply into her eyes. She could see every fleck of gold and green in his intensely blue irises, and the question coming from his soul. Before she could take another breath, he covered her mouth with his.

She lost her breath as his tongue pressed past the barrier of her teeth and mated with hers. The intensity of the kiss made her dizzy and bared her heart until she felt completely exposed and naked before him. There was nowhere to hide, and she couldn't move away.

It was the sweetest, most intoxicating moment of her life. The way he touched her felt so right, so perfect, and stirred her on such a profound level. She hadn't even known she was capable of such depths, and the fact he brought it out astounded her.

She didn't even *like* him! Or did she?

She heard his breath trembling as he lifted his head from hers. Time stood still. Fire glowed in his eyes.

"Your lips . . . Cassie . . . I don't know . . ." he whispered when he could find his voice.

Her whole body trembled and she tried to pull away. She wanted to say something light to defuse the situation, but nothing came to her. All she could do was concentrate on standing up. His hands on her arms prevented her from falling, but she struggled with the feeling of vulnerability.

"Always so strong, aren't you, Cassie?" he asked as if reading her mind.

"Strength is something I have acquired in times of adversity."

He chuckled. "I'd wager you were born strong. Your character can't have changed that much."

"Perhaps not, but it has been honed over time, and

since James died, my strength has been tested repeatedly."

"You have all those sterling qualities I lack," he muttered and finally released her. She felt bereft of his closeness, not knowing what to say. She had carped too much on him to take it all back now.

"There's no reason to continue this conversation." She reached for her umbrella. Her hand shook and she slammed the door on the vulnerability in her heart. "Let's fetch Giselle and head back to the house."

Twelve

They returned to Fairweather. Mr. Bunney was silent throughout the trip, starlight shining in his eyes. He had an expression of heavenly bliss on his face and a perpetual smile on his lips.

Dylan tried to pull him into a conversation, but Eddie only replied in monosyllables. Dylan had his own emotions to think about. Kissing Cassie and feeling such a strong connection had truly rocked his very foundation, bared his soul as nothing else had been able to do. Her smile, her apprehension, the confusion in her eyes as he kissed her had forever changed his life. How could a moment of closeness change one's life so totally?

Cupid must be enjoying floating around the vicinity of Fairweather, he thought, feeling helpless to deal with the situation. It was unlikely that Cassie wanted anything to do with him. After this last kiss, she probably would not speak with him again.

"I thought we'd never find our way out of the maze," Hazel said for the fifth time since they had entered the carriage. "All that walking almost killed me!"

"Me, too," Hermione chimed in.

"I believe 'twas excessively rude of Lady Pender

to get us all lost in the maze," Hazel continued. She slapped Dylan's arm lightly. "And *you,* young whippersnapper, suggested the whole ordeal."

"I thought the idea was a stroke of brilliance," Mr. Bunney said dreamily.

"I have no idea what you're talking about," Hazel said peevishly. "All I know is that my feet are burning up and my head is pounding. The sun could very easily have put an end to me. And to Hermione."

"When we get home, I'll arrange for a basin of cool water for your feet," Cassie said.

"I can just stick them in one of the buckets for the roof leaks," Hazel said, a nasty edge in her voice. "Not that I'm not grateful for the roof over my head. And so is Hermione."

No one answered her tirade.

"And that poor Lady Cutting, she got blisters all over her feet, and you should've seen the size of her bunions. I don't know how she walks at all. Such a calamity. We never should have accepted the invitation."

"Wild horses could not have kept you away," Cassie said, her voice tired.

Dylan gave her a searching glance, but she averted her eyes.

"You're young, Cassie, and I'm willing to wager you have healthy feet. I declare Lady Pender led us down the wrong path on purpose, then disappeared. If it hadn't been for Dylan we would still be lost looking for the exit—or dead," Hazel rattled on.

The carriage hit a bump in the lane and Hermione cried out. "My poor head!"

Dylan felt sorry that the old ladies had suffered due to his schemes, but the look on Eddie's face compensated for everything.

"Lady Cutting was livid, of course, when she realized Giselle had been whisked away," Hazel continued her monologue. "Not that she'll say anything to Mr. Duggan, who won't give her anything but grief. Of course she can't *prove* Giselle was with Mr. Bunney, as Cassie brought her out of the maze. But we all *know* Mr. Bunney didn't waste the opportunity to speak to Giselle."

She gave Mr. Bunney a penetrating look. He only heaved a trembling sigh and stared vacantly into space.

"Everyone is very quiet," Hazel complained. "I try to keep up a polite conversation, but I guess it's too much to expect a polite response back."

"We're all tired, I'm sure," Cassie said. "A large delicious meal and then all that exercise in the sun will take the strength out of anyone."

The topic of the dowager's maze dwindled as there was nothing more to say on the matter. Dylan knew the Elderberry twins would never venture back into it.

They arrived back at Fairweather in uncomfortable silence.

Mrs. Granger met them on the front steps just as soon as they had alighted from the carriage.

"There has been another break-in, this one in broad daylight," she cried, her face creased with worry. "I didn't hear anything, nor did Ned. They pulled out everything in the study and tossed all the papers in the desk all over the floor. The furniture is overturned and broken in places."

Dylan saw red. "By God, that man is insane," he shouted. "I don't know what the Duggans have against me, but I'll find out today. Enough's enough!" He stormed into the house and inspected the damage.

Cassie entered right behind him, and her eyes widened in horror. She clapped her hand to her mouth as if to stifle a scream. The furniture had not been worth much, but the destruction was a threat against their very lives.

"I'm going to have it out with Mr. Duggan," he said, his temples pounding with anger.

Her eyes looked dark and defenseless. "Be careful, Dylan."

Somehow he felt responsible for everything, felt her safety and everyone else's depended on him. His family. This strange conglomeration of people had somehow become his family, and so quickly. He didn't know how, but it had happened. Fairweather had been a ship without a rudder until he inherited it. Without Cassie, it would've been totally destroyed, but somehow she'd held it all together in the last year.

He clasped her shoulders lightly, and she stiffened immediately. The suspicion in her eyes hurt him.

"I just want to say thank you for caring about Fairweather and protecting it the best way you could, Cassie. There's no way I can repay you for your responsibility and insights."

Hope lit her eyes. "Fairweather deserves a better fate than she's had so far. She's a grand old lady."

A sudden cold draft flew through the open window, and Dylan felt a chill up his spine. "You're right. Fairweather deserves to rise in full dignity."

"So you are dedicated to restoring the estate?"

He paused. "Was there ever any doubt in you mind about that?"

She pursed her lips in thought. "I . . . don't know. I . . . suppose I never believed you would desert her—your childhood home."

"At one time I would have," he said and meant

it. "And not that long ago. Fairweather meant nothing to me except old memories, most of them hazy at best."

"Things change sometimes when we least expect them to," she said. She moved away from him and started picking up the books strewn over the floor and the ruined portrait of Captain Brooks.

"You don't have to do that, Cassie. Ned can bring his nephews in here to sort out the chaos."

She hesitated as if unsure of what to do. "It's difficult to look at this and not do something about it."

"Yes, but I don't want to see you upset, Cassie. Ned can handle it."

She put down the books in her hands. "I'll go upstairs and rest for a while," she said and left the room.

Dylan looked at her back as she disappeared and felt frustration rise within, and with it his anger. Filled with purpose, he walked outside, heading for the stables to collect Joker, his horse.

Danger, danger, signaled every cell in Cassie's body. Dylan's presence had overpowered her reason, the very essence of her. His kiss had robbed her of every coherent thought, and she suspected her ability to think clearly had been removed permanently.

She had dissolved into a million tiny pieces, and she feared they would never come together as they had been before. His kiss had changed her life, as surely as the sun rose every morning over the Channel.

His existence at Fairweather was changing the very fabric of everything, and everybody. The others had begun to look to Dylan for advice.

She fled into her room and closed the door behind her. Leaning her back against the wood, she closed her eyes and sighed. Why didn't the others see the obvious?

Dylan would never change. Gambling was in his blood, and the fact he'd never sought to alter his life was enough proof that he had no desire, no urge to transform.

She sat on the edge of her bed. She hadn't felt this low since her father passed away. A groan built in her throat, and she pressed a pillow against her face to cry out her frustration.

The expression made her feel better, and she went to brush her hair. She put it back up into a thick chignon and dressed in an old gown. Dylan had asked her not to be involved with the disruption in the library, but she had to try to figure out if the intruders had taken something—or found something.

There was no doubt in her mind that the person or persons who had broken in were connected to the man Ripple had attacked the other night.

She went downstairs and found Ned and his nephews carrying broken furniture from the room.

"How will we ever replace these things?" she asked as the wing chair, from which stuffing protruded in tatters, was borne outside. Ned's stalwart nephews only gave her a questioning glance, but Ned scratched his head and stared at the heap on the floor.

"That's a good question an' all," he said. "Costs a mint to order new pieces. Whoever did this 'as no respect for other people's property."

"That's right." Cassie started lifting broken pieces from the floor. "What I don't understand is why they had to destroy the things—unless they expected to find something hidden inside."

"Aye, that's possible," Ned said and nudged a broken chair leg with his heavy boot. "I'd say they didn't find it, though."

"Why?"

"If they had, they wouldn't have destroyed everything."

"Unless they had a streak of vindictiveness," she said.

"Aye, but we don't 'ave any enemies exceptin'—"

"—Mr. Duggan," she filled in.

Ned nodded, his face creased in serious lines. He gave her a guarded look, as if worrying what she planned to do about it.

"I will not go into battle with Mr. Duggan," she assured him, "but I can't vouch for Mr. Wenthaven."

" 'E's not goin' to take this layin' down," Ned said ominously.

Cassie knew that to be a statement of truth. She started sorting through the books, hoping to find something that would tell her about the intruders.

One hour later, she felt both sweaty and thirsty. Dust hovered in the air, and she had come no closer to finding any answers. She began to put the books back into the bookshelves on both sides of the fireplace. They snagged on a knot in the wood, and she had to replace some as they fell down again. She wished something new had come to light, but these were the same old books she'd already gone through in the past.

"Mrs. Wenthaven," Ned said, looking around the room. "Tom and Sid have carried out the last pieces. Couldn't find a thing."

"Neither could I."

"The room looks bleak, doesn't it?"

"All the flaws on the walls and floor are evident without the furniture, aren't they?"

Ned nodded. "Captain Brooks wouldn't be pleased if 'e saw what this place 'as come to."

Cassie looked out the window, almost expecting the cold breeze to sweep in as it usually did when the captain's name was mentioned. Nothing happened, and she wondered if she was losing her mind. "Captain Brooks died one hundred and fifty years ago, Ned."

"Some say 'e did, some say 'e didn't."

"Don't be ridiculous," she snapped. She looked at the tidy rows of books and the shelves that had warped over time. Someone had lovingly carved clusters of fruit in the mantel above the shelves, and the paint had chipped off the grapes and the apples, leaving darker spots where rot had taken hold.

She would see to it that the bookshelves were restored with a loving touch. Fairweather needed so much work. It would take years to restore.

She glanced out the open window again, but nothing moved. A heaviness hung over the area, as if a storm tried to gather in the massive clouds grouped together along.

She wondered if the storm would catch Dylan as he rode along.

Rainstorms were the last thing on Dylan's mind as his horse galloped up the long drive to Duggan's mansion. Poplars lined the winding lane, and beautiful groves of trees had been planted all over the grounds, but he wasn't in the mood to admire the landscape.

"Damn you, Duggan," he muttered under his

breath as he rode up to the front entrance and jumped off his mount. He ran up the shallow stone steps and banged on the massive door.

A footman answered the call and gave Dylan a look full of fear. "Mr. Wenthaven? I regret to tell you—"

"Get out of my way," Dylan snapped and pushed past the startled servant.

The butler appeared, his back stiff with disapproval. "Mr. Duggan is not at home."

"I shall see for myself." Dylan headed toward the library where he'd kissed Cassie in the darkness. He flung the door open, but the room was empty.

He listened for sounds and heard voices in the dining room, then recognized Lady Cutting's high tones. Possibly she was still complaining about the Dowager Lady Pender's tea party, leaving out the most important parts in the maze, of course.

Dylan threw the door wide and stepped inside. Julius Duggan, Lady Cutting, and Giselle sat around the table sharing the evening meal. Lady Cutting clapped her hand over her mouth to suppress a squeal, and Giselle's eyes widened in shock. Mr. Duggan's face took on a thunderous expression.

"What are you doing in my house?" he barked.

"I'm not leaving until I have some answers," Dylan shouted. "Your people have trampled all over my property and destroyed my furniture, and I want to know why. There's no doubt you're behind the whole scheme. How dare you invade my privacy in this manner?" Dylan was so angry he barely could get the words out.

"What?"

"Don't pretend you don't know what I'm talking about," Dylan shouted at the top of his lungs.

Lady Cutting pulled Giselle with her and escaped

through the open terrace doors. No doubt she would listen from the safety of some distance, Dylan thought sourly.

"I'm going to run you through," Mr. Duggan screamed, his face purple with rage as he pushed back his chair and leaned over the table. The chair fell to the floor with a crash.

"I don't see a sword at your side, and I don't intend to fight it out. I want an explanation about why you feel this hostility toward my family. I haven't done anything. In fact, I barely know you, seeing as I've spent very little time at Fairweather. Your animosity is insane! I demand an explanation."

Mr. Duggan tried to get some words out, but his lips would not cooperate as rage got the better of him. He slumped back into his chair. He drank some water, and Dylan waited, every muscle in his body knotted with tension.

"Well!" Mr. Duggan slammed his fist into the table so hard the silverware jangled. "You want an explanation? First of all, Fairweather is a terrible eyesore and not getting any better with time. All my life I've struggled, first with your parents, then with Seffington, to purchase the property so it wouldn't darken my view of the Channel. Second, you harbor a gabble of eccentrics at Fairweather who have nothing better to do than spy on my people and gossip. I don't know where you found these ragged tenants, but they won't do!"

"Who lives at Fairweather is my responsibility, not yours," Dylan said hotly.

"And that sister-in-law of yours is a constant thorn in my side. She had the audacity to tell me she's your steward. That's the most ridiculous thing I've ever heard."

"I did hire Mrs. Wenthaven as my steward, but that was before I decided to take the reins of running Fairweather myself. Besides, you can't find fault with her. She's done everything in her power to keep Fairweather from falling down."

"It may have been a good thing to have it fall down!" Mr. Duggan cried. "It needs to be torn down and the grounds leveled and planted over."

"I intend to restore it," Dylan said coldly.

"*What!* Where are *you* going to get the funds to restore Fairweather? 'Twill take a fortune, and a wasted effort for certain."

"It depends on one's views. Fairweather means something to me. It represents roots, family history."

"Ah! Family history, is it?" Mr. Duggan asked scathingly. "Your history is so cursed and riddled with deceit and crime that it's something you should want to bury deeply and never dig up again."

"I know that old history of Captain Brooks and his piracy, but my parents, grandparents, and Seffington were all law-abiding and honest people."

"That fact doesn't take away the darkness which was perpetrated in the far past. It still has consequences today."

"Are you saying whatever Captain Brooks and those of his era did have an impact on your family today?" Dylan couldn't believe his ears. Duggan evidently presumed this if his vehement expression spoke the truth.

"Captain Brooks murdered my ancestor, the captain of the Duggan ship, and stole his fortune. If that isn't enough for a feud, I don't know what is."

Thirteen

"Murder?" Dylan asked, flabbergasted. "I knew about the robbery and the burning, but there's no indication—"

"I have two written accounts that speak of this. Not only did my ancestor lose his life, he lost everything—thanks to Captain Brooks, who used the funds to build Fairweather."

Mr. Duggan's color had abated somewhat, and Dylan felt his own anger slowly dissipating.

"Whatever Captain Brooks accomplished was through murder and thievery. As far as I know, he wasn't very good at piracy on the seas, not to a point where he would've made a fortune the size it took to build Fairweather."

"That is speculation," Dylan said stiffly.

"What fortune we built in my family was through honest hard labor building ships," Mr. Duggan said, his voice flattening with exhaustion. "We have always lived in this spot, but we lost fortunes, and rebuilt them."

He pointed a rigid finger at Dylan. "Your ancestor was a crook of the worst kind, and I want to see Fairweather gone. Then I shall have peace. You can go and build your empire somewhere else, young man."

"I have as much of a right to live here as you do. My history goes back long before Captain Brooks, and I'm sure the land and the buildings that went before Fairweather were acquired with total honesty."

"You would say that, wouldn't you? But that irresponsible streak runs in your blood. If Fairweather stays with you, I'll be plagued for the rest of my life with the sight of that . . . *heap!*"

"Sometimes we have to learn how to bend a little," Dylan said. "I've had enough of this drivel. From now on, stay off my property. If I see any of your people lurking about, I will shoot. It's not an empty threat." Dylan headed back toward the front entrance.

"Murderer!" Mr. Duggan shouted behind him. "Just like your ancestors."

Fuming, Dylan returned to Fairweather and went in search of Cassie. He found her dusting and placing the last books on the shelves in the library. The room looked bare, and she was alone.

Her old gown was covered with dust, and her hair had come undone from the chignon and was curling beguilingly around her face. She had never looked more beautiful, in his opinion, and his heart skipped a beat.

He longed to sweep her into his arms and hold her tight, but he didn't touch her, knowing she would step away.

"I see Mr. Duggan didn't shoot you," she said with a wry smile.

"He wanted to," Dylan said, feeling himself relaxing in her presence. He drew a long breath and told her everything Mr. Duggan had said.

"We know from Captain Brooks's own journal he'd stolen the Duggan fortune, but I haven't seen an account of any murders." She looked thoughtfully into the distance. "Not that it would be out of the question. Anyone who is capable of piracy is capable of cold-blooded killings. Perhaps Captain Brooks was afraid of writing about it. Unless he used it as some sort of confession."

"Yes, I agree with that," Dylan said thoughtfully. "I'd say Mr. Duggan won't give up his goal to erase Fairweather from the face of the earth. Not only because of some ancient wrongdoing, but of what is happening this day here—the decay, the disorder." He refrained from repeating the unkind words Duggan had spoken of Cassie and the others.

"I understand that. Mr. Duggan is a fanatic about his grounds and his estate. There's not one blade of grass that dares to grow crooked on that property."

Dylan could not help but laugh. "Well put, Cassie." He looked at her for a long moment. "I intend to fight him. Will you stand by me?"

She glanced away, clearly embarrassed. "I don't know everything such a proposition entails, but I'll fight for the future of Fairweather. That is the least I can do to repay Seffington's kindness for letting me stay here when I had nowhere to go."

"*I* am asking you, Cassie. This has nothing to do with Seffington's kindness. Besides, he never did anything charitable unless he could gain something from it. He gained a steward of sorts with you."

She seemed uncomfortable, but then accepted. "Yes, I'll stand by you." She glanced at the books on the shelves. "What I don't understand is why Mr.

Duggan would want to snoop around Fairweather if all he wants is to buy it and erase it."

"Yes, that was something I never got an answer to, but I left before we came to blows."

"I'm certain he wouldn't have told you the truth. If he could come right out and speak to you, there would be no need for skulduggery."

"You're right, of course." He rubbed his jaw and looked around the empty room. "We have something he wants."

The wind fluttered the curtain by the open window, gained in strength, and blew through the room. The curtain flapped, and the smell of rain came to Dylan's nose. "A storm is brewing."

" 'Tis hot tonight. The atmosphere needs to release before we all suffocate."

"There may be more than the weather that makes the atmosphere thick and unbearable." He longed desperately to sweep her into his arms and kiss her until she went soft and pliant, but of course that would happen only in his mind.

"You're making assumptions," she said. "If you're hot, there's always the cove on the beach where you can cool off in the water. Just be careful of the undercurrents."

"I'm well aware of the undercurrents," he said, his voice deepening with need.

She blushed a deep rose and patted her wayward curls with a trembling hand. There was no mistaking the undercurrents there, he thought, suddenly elated that she cared enough to become uncomfortable. If she didn't care, she would've just given him one of those cool level stares and walked out of the room. As it was, she looked as if she was near fainting.

He reached out and removed her hand from her hair and wound the brown gleaming curls behind her ear. Her gaze darted to his face and away, then back, then away. He pulled the pad of his thumb across her lips, savoring the softness. When she didn't move away, he leaned toward her and planted the lightest of kisses on her mouth, then pulled back.

Time stood still as their gazes met and melted together in so many unspoken words. In the next breath, she whirled around and ran from the room.

Dylan found he could barely breathe, and when the storm arrived outside, he closed his eyes and thanked the forces that brought relief. Rain spattered over the foliage outside and trickled down the broken spouts along the eaves.

A cool breeze stirred the leaves, and he breathed deeply. He prayed he would be strong enough to take on the giant undertaking that was Fairweather.

Cassie fled to her bedroom for the second time that day, wondering if she would ever find a way to get past the feelings Dylan had stirred up in her.

Merlin lay curled up on the bed, and she caressed the ginger cat, who had not one care in the world. He purred and stretched long. "What do you know of the turmoil of man?" she whispered.

Merlin seemed to say with his slitted eyes that he saw through everything but still didn't care.

When she'd calmed down a little, she looked for Captain Brooks's journal, which she'd put under her bed. She leaned back against the pillows, and Merlin fitted himself comfortably against her thigh and continued to purr in a comforting fashion. Why a cat's purr could feel so comforting she could not explain, but she scratched his ears as she sought the place in the journal where she'd placed a marker.

She decided to move toward the end of the diary to see if there had been any mention of Captain Brooks's murderous deeds. She doubted it greatly, but as she was reading she found more and more detail about the night the Duggan ship had been looted.

After half an hour of deciphering crabby handwriting, she found, to her surprise, a paragraph that showed a great deal of agitation.

It appeared the captain *had* killed the Duggan ancestor in cold blood. No wonder he couldn't find peace in heaven, she thought. He also went on to describe what a thorn in his side the Duggan ancestor had been as they always feuded about adjoining land. The acrimony hadn't been sudden. Captain Brooks had brutally finalized a lifelong battle.

She went back, searching through the tightly written script for more clues. Maybe the captain could help her discover why Mr. Duggan sent in people to destroy the furniture at Fairweather if he was interested only in erasing Fairweather.

"I'm certain it has to do with the treasure, but what kind of treasure are we looking for, Merlin?" she asked aloud. "Money? Jewelry? Old weapons?"

She decided to go back up to the attic and look around. Perhaps she'd missed something the last time she went upstairs to fetch the journal. Not that she'd searched very thoroughly. The leaks in the roof had distracted her.

Hoping she wouldn't run into Dylan or the others, she hurried up the rickety stairs to the attic and opened the creaky door. The same musty smell as always assaulted her nostrils, and the stains of the leaks had spread to a much larger area. She studied the damage the last heavy rains had made. Before long this corner of the roof would cave in.

She started with the first trunk, already disliking the idea as she worried what kind of furry creatures she might come across. Everything ought to be brought down and aired out or burned. So many of the old clothes had turned into useless piles of mold and rot.

She found a broken broom handle and sorted through the contents of three trunks without finding anything of the slightest interest.

The air had gotten increasingly colder. The rain must've brought a change to the atmosphere. The heaviness was gone, and she felt relieved after a long day of tension.

The fourth trunk held nothing but books, and she'd already gone through those. No one could've hid a treasure in this moldy pile, she thought.

Some baskets had been stacked against the wall and she searched those, finding nothing but spiders.

"Nothing at all, but what could I expect?" she said out loud. One thing she hadn't studied were the walls. As she had downstairs, she looked for any unusual cracks or formations in the wood that might conceal a hiding place, but mostly every beam and post were fully revealed. Unless some hole had been carved into the beams, there was no hope.

She went over every area with much care, finding absolutely nothing that piqued her interest. Tired and dustier than ever, she decided to end her search and return downstairs. At least she had tried.

She decided to walk downstairs to heat some water in the kitchen for a bath. In the foyer, that icy-cold air surrounded her, and she immediately thought of the ghost.

"I'm not going to run away," she whispered. "What do you want?" She looked around to see if anyone had witnessed her speaking to thin air, but no movement came from the rooms around her.

The icy air swirled around her, reminding her of the whirlwinds of dust she sometimes saw on the lane leading to the house. This appeared a lot bigger, and for a moment she panicked. Ripple would not panic, she thought. Ripple would just accept it and honor its existence.

"What do you want?" she repeated, and felt as if the ghost—yes, she finally dared to accept the possibility of a ghost—were tugging at her to move in the direction of the study. She took a few steps and sensed the distinct movement of the air around her.

Desperately looking around, she wondered if the ancient pirate would become visible, and the thought frightened her.

"I've had enough of this," she said, and fled to the kitchen, where Mrs. Granger was up to her elbows in flour. The familiar sight comforted Cassie. She closed the door to the rest of the house with a slam.

"You look like ye've seen a ghost," Mrs. Granger said, and Cassie could've screamed with the irony of it all.

"Perhaps I did," she replied and sank down on a chair by the table, exhausted.

"You never!" Mrs. Granger's eyes grew round. "I thought ye didn't believe in them."

"I don't," Cassie said, disgusted with everything all of a sudden.

The infant boy gurgled in his basket by the hearth,

and she went to pick him up. He smelled sweetly of milk and baby skin, and she admired his happy toothless grin. *Here is someone who knows how to enjoy the moment,* she thought. No worries at all; no care whether the roof would cave in or the neighbors would start a war.

He opened his beautiful blue eyes and looked right into hers. This could've been her son if . . . She didn't even bother to finish the thought.

"Ye're growin' mighty fond of the tyke, aren't you, Mrs. Wenthaven?"

She could not hide from Mrs. Granger's shrewd eyes. "I suppose you're right," she confessed. "How can you resist?"

"It won't do to become attached," Mrs. Granger said. "When they find the mother, the tyke has to go."

Cassie nodded her head. "Yes . . . I suppose he would have to." She lifted him into the air as he cooed with happiness. She would miss him. "I would name him Christopher," she said. "Such a good robust name."

"Aye, but he should have his father's name, don't you think?"

"Not if the mother is unwed."

"Ye've already adopted him, haven't you, Mrs. Wenthaven?"

"It wouldn't be such a bad idea, but I have no resources with which to care for an infant. He needs his mother more than anything."

"Aye, the boy's in a difficult spot." Mrs. Granger kneaded the dough on the workbench, and Cassie could almost taste the fresh bread on her tongue already. Mrs. Granger surely was a great cook.

"Mr. Wenthaven has a tenderness for the boy as

well," the older woman continued, "seeing as the baby might be family." Mrs. Granger clamped her mouth shut, and Cassie knew that was all she would say. She had said too much already.

Fourteen

"And you should see the sloth of those workmen!" Hazel said one morning to Cassie after her walk. One week had passed since her encounter with the ghost, and workmen had invaded Fairweather. They were in the process of tearing off the roof, and Cassie couldn't find any place to hide from the noise and upheaval.

"You would think they are beggars the way they dress. Tatters, I tell you! Indecent the way they expose—"

"Hazel, I have no doubt you're right, but I have no desire to verify your accusations. And besides, tearing off the old roof is filthy work. You can't expect them to be wearing their Sunday best."

Hazel's nose went up a notch and she sniffed. "No, I'm not asking for that, only common decency so one can take one's morning walk without blushing. I am full of fear of where this will all lead."

Cassie laughed. " 'Twill lead to a new roof, Hazel, and great improvement."

Dylan had wasted no time bringing in a crew and ordering a pile of lumber that would replace the damaged wood structures. When he decided on something, he certainly dedicated himself with full force.

The only cloud on the otherwise sunny skies was the fact that gambling money had financed the venture, and Cassie couldn't forget that.

"Yes, I suppose it will," Hazel agreed reluctantly. "Have you seen Dylan and Mr. Bunney this morning? They are always giving out advice to the foreman where none is desired."

"Makes them feel important," Hazel said and put down her parasol, her gloves, and her hat on a chair in the dining room where Cassie was finishing her morning coffee. "Haven't laid eyes on either one of them." The older woman poured herself a cup of tea and sat down at the table. "Gentlemen have a need to feel important," she added. "Have to push themselves forward at every turn."

"Is that so?" Cassie wondered what kind of exposure Hazel had had to gentlemen in the past. Not much, she decided.

"My father always thought he knew the answers to everything, and didn't hesitate to tell us so."

"Yes . . . I suppose they can be quite unreasonable at times. If gainsaid, they are thrown into conflict."

"Take Mr. Bunney for instance," Hazel said in a voice laced with disgust. "I *warned* him not to try to see Miss Duggan whilst she's under Mr. Duggan's roof. Nothing good will ever come of trying that, only calamities. Would he listen to me? No, of course not. He's even now plotting how to spirit Miss Duggan off to Gretna Green for one of those harum-scarum clandestine weddings."

Cassie felt a wave of alarm. "Did he actually tell you that?"

Hazel pursed her lips, as if carefully choosing her

words. "Not exactly, but I *know*. He's in for nothing but trouble."

Eddie Bunney had disappeared, Dylan noticed as he saddled his horse for a morning ride. Perhaps Eddie had decided to leave due to the noise and the commotion around Fairweather. The packing of his trunks would take Ripple a day or two, Dylan mused, smiling as he thought of his friend's extensive wardrobe. Eddie had always been particular about his apparel.

He patted the hilt of his sword, which he'd taken to wearing since his argument with Mr. Duggan, rode down the drive and stopped to look back at Fairweather. Part of the roof had been torn off, and the mansion was a sorry sight. It had to get worse before it got better, he thought. The change, however ugly, felt good.

The morning dew clung to all the leaves and grasses, spinning a magical web over the meadows. As he continued on his ride, birds sang all around him. A blessed morning, he thought. The only thing missing was Cassie riding beside him.

After spending several sleepless nights, he had come to the realization that he'd fallen deeply in love with her. The understanding pained him no end. He didn't want to need her in his life, and he detested the idea of pain if she rejected him.

If one loved someone and they left, as Dermott had, one went through a lot of pain. Somehow love always connected to pain on some level. Even the ecstasy of that touching of souls in a kiss held an element of suffering; at some point, one would have to let go of that kiss.

You are morose, he thought as he turned down the path between his property and Mr. Duggan's. He liked this area the best, with its aspen copses and rolling hills. He guessed this had been the land over which the Brookses and the Duggans had fought in the old times. There hadn't been any land feuds that he was aware of for a long time.

From the top of those hills, he could see out over the Channel and its ever-changing vistas. Here he could feel he was part of the Sussex earth, that his roots went deep into this land, something he appreciated more every day. He'd been at loose ends most of his life. Dermott had never had the chance to experience this.

He rode along the back of Duggan's property. Shrubs and the occasional oak tree flourished here, and as he was about to head into the hills, he heard the sound of angry voices.

"You scoundrel! You can't deny I caught you red-handed courting my daughter on the terrace of my own house!"

Dylan would've recognized that choleric voice anywhere. Mr. Duggan. And Eddie.

"I have only the highest intentions for Miss Duggan, and she knows that. It's more than I can ever say of you, Mr. Duggan. You don't even have the decency to hear me out." Eddie sounded peevish, Dylan thought, and that would incense Mr. Duggan beyond rage.

He rode up to the small clearing just as Mr. Duggan tossed a sword to Eddie.

"Defend yourself!"

How Eddie thought he would be able to fight with one of his arms still in a sling was beyond Dylan.

The swords clanged together as they moved out of

the *en garde* position and commenced battle, no seconds in sight.

Dylan wanted to halt the action, but it might mean injury to his friend. He jumped off his horse and tied the reins to a sapling at the edge of the clearing.

"You wretch," Mr. Duggan shouted. "I'll run you through as surely as the sun rises for ever daring to send a glance in my daughter's direction."

His face was turning purple, Dylan noted. The man had no patience. Putting his hand on the hilt of his sword, he was ready to jump to Eddie's assistance, should he need it. Eddie had always been quick on his feet. He danced around the older man, jabbing and feinting. Mr. Duggan didn't have the agility, but his sword was true. Eddie had a worthy opponent.

"I'm in love with your daughter, Mr. Duggan. What's so criminal about that?" Eddie cried.

"She deserves a lot better than you—a gambler and a fop without two groats to rub together. My Giselle deserves a gentleman, not someone from the dregs of society."

"My grandparents were the Duke and Duchess of Lorindale, eminent people in their time, and I'm related to three earls and a viscount." Eddie was losing his breath as he jumped and slid on the grass.

All that indulgence at the table was taking its toll, Dylan thought. Eddie liked wine with his dinner.

It all happened so fast. Mr. Duggan lunged, catching Eddie unaware. The tip of Duggan's sword sliced through the sleeve of Eddie's sword arm and bored a hole through his bicep. Eddie shouted in pain and fell to his knees.

Mr. Duggan stepped back, panting heavily. He leaned against a tree trunk to catch his breath. "I should run you through while I have the chance," he said hoarsely.

Dylan knew he was good for this threat and stepped forward. "You'll have to fight me before you kill him," he demanded, pulling out his weapon.

Mr. Duggan's expression was murderous. *"You!* How dare you step foot on my property?"

"I heard your voices, and you know duels are illegal. I don't believe anything can be solved with swords."

"I honestly don't care what you think, Mr. Wenthaven." Mr. Duggan put his weapon back into its scabbard and gave Eddie a glance full of loathing. "If I as much as catch a sight of you anywhere on my property, I will shoot you. Stay away from my daughter, now and forever!"

Giving Dylan an angry look, he stalked off along a path among the trees.

Dylan went to help Eddie to his feet.

"Oooh—aaoo," Eddie cried, blood streaming down his sleeve. Dylan tore off the ruined fabric, exposing the wound. He pulled off his neckcloth and bound it tightly around the wound.

"It was incredibly mutton-headed to visit Miss Duggan in broad daylight," he admonished. "You knew you couldn't avoid Duggan, and I'm sure you knew he would call you out."

Eddie grimaced, sweat running down his pale face. "I just couldn't stay . . . away," he blurted out, his voice faltering. "She's in my blood—"

"—and you can't think of anything else," Dylan filled in.

"No."

Dylan led his friend to his own horse. Eddie's mount had to be somewhere, but he could wait. Eddie climbed into the saddle with difficulty, using the arm that had almost healed. Obviously he wrenched it and gave an agonizing howl.

Both arms now hung limp at his sides, and Dylan had never seen a more pitiful sight. He shook his head and inserted the arm back into its black sling, then fashioned another from Eddie's neckcloth.

Eddie, now wearing both arms in slings, looked as if he wanted to cry. He struggled with his emotions as Dylan led the horse out of the clearing and back onto Fairweather property.

When they returned to the house, Hazel and Hermione met them in the foyer, their hands clapped to their mouths in distress.

"Oh, my dear Mr. Bunney," Hazel exclaimed.

"Oh, dear," Hermione whispered.

"I shall wear my badge of battle with pride," Eddie said, trying for a triumphant smile, which failed miserably.

Cassie joined them, exclaiming her surprise. "What happened?"

Dylan explained, and she immediately wanted to send for the doctor.

"No!" Eddie cried. "No sawbones. I shall have Ripple bandage my arm, and that'll be the end of it."

"How are you going to eat with both hands out of commission?" Hazel asked.

"I'm counting on my friends to help me," Eddie said, and Dylan looked toward the ceiling, asking for strength.

"I'm sure these ladies are full of compassion, but I'm not," Dylan said, disgusted. "Total stupidity put you into this position, and I refuse to suffer along with you."

Eddie gave him a mournful look, and Dylan had had enough of all this moping, moaning, sighing, and incessant talk about *love.* "You can eat like a dog for all I care," he said, "right off the plate."

"Such cruelty," Eddie said and turned his theatrical attention to the ladies.

You would think it would hurt too much to get into the melodrama of the situation, Dylan thought and went in search of Ripple. That stalwart man was taking a nap in a chair in Eddie's bedroom, his head leaning against the armoire.

He jumped as Dylan said his name. "Ah! . . . Mr. Wenthaven. I had the most horrible dream about my employer."

"I'm afraid it's come true, Ripple. You need to clean and bandage a sword wound—in his other arm."

Ripple's eyes grew round. "His *other* arm? Gorblimey, you would think he'd be a little more prudent than that." The man scuttled around and gathered up scissors, bandages, a black silk neckcloth, and a bottle of brandy. "He'll need some to fortify himself, and I'll use some to cleanse the wound."

"We're going to have to listen to Eddie claiming he's at death's door," Dylan said, still annoyed his friend had not shown more sense. "Mayhap it would've been a good thing if Mr. Duggan had run him through."

Ripple looked shocked. "Mr. Wenthaven!"

Dylan shook his head and left the room. Downstairs, Eddie was surrounded by his court of ladies in the dining room, where he sat in a chair with cushions propped behind him and each arm cradled on a pillow.

Ripple set to work cutting away the rest of the

fabric around the wound, and Hermione almost fainted. Cassie had to waft a bottle of smelling salts under her nose, then lead her to her bedchamber.

Dylan decided he'd had enough. He left the house and went to the rose arbor in the back, where he'd first noticed how beguilingly Cassie's curls framed her face.

So much had happened in such a short time. When Seffington died, his whole life had changed. Maybe the old bleater had seen something in him he never saw himself—a seed, a hope for the future.

"Ripple is fully in charge," Cassie said behind him. "There's never a dull moment since Mr. Bunney arrived at Fairweather."

He turned around and there she stood, the woman, the sister-in-law he'd fallen in love with. His heart hammered crazily in his chest. "Eddie should've tread the boards; everything he does is drama."

"I had enough of it," she said simply.

"So did I. We'll never hear the end of the moaning and groaning now, especially since he'll be separated from his beloved."

"The wound in his arm looks rather serious, but I'd say the wound in his heart will be harder to heal. Giselle will never be his—unless a miracle happens."

"Miracles have been known to happen at times, but they are rare. Besides, I'm not sure Eddie has done anything to *deserve* a miracle."

"Sometimes they are bestowed randomly, without any obvious reason," she said.

Silence hovered between them, and Dylan longed to sweep her into his arms, but he sensed he would be rebuffed. He sought desperately for something to say, but could think of nothing even slightly interesting.

"The workmen are hardworking and diligent," she said. "At this rate, we'll have a new roof soon."

"You say 'we.' I didn't think you approved of this venture, seeing as it was ventured with tainted money."

She blushed and looked away. "The roof is still what's important. Without it, Fairweather doesn't have a chance."

"I'm glad you see that." He longed to say so much more, to explain about the gambling, but no words came to his lips. He couldn't take any more arguments or rebuffs, not when his efforts felt good and right.

They stood in the silence, hesitant.

She spoke first. "What are your plans after the roof?"

"I think the outside work needs to be done first. The walls must be rebuilt and patched, the foundation straightened and renovated. Then we can move the work inside, wholly restoring one room at a time."

"The windows need to be replaced as well."

"Your suggestion is sound, Cassie. Perhaps we should sit down and write a plan for the whole restoration."

"Together?"

"I need your advice, Cassie. With your superior brain, no cracks will go unfilled, no repairs forgotten." He smiled. "I'd be lost without you."

"Nonsense. You'll be very much in charge. I'll be leaving just as soon as I hear from the family up north who needs a governess."

Dylan felt as if a fist had slammed into his stomach. It was unthinkable that Cassie would leave. "You wrote to them?"

"Yes, right after I realized my position as steward here was unrealistic."

"I see." He noticed the stubborn set of her jaw. "If you leave, the backbone of this place will be gone."

She studied his face intently for any falsity, but he meant every word.

"Are you saying you don't have any stability?" she probed, her eyes so serious he could barely look at her.

"The situations around me never inspired stability. I've lived from day to day, and I still do, but with Fairweather I have a future."

"But no funds. How do you intend—"

"Leave that up to me," he interrupted forcefully. "I've never had problems providing, and I never will. I've relied on my wits for a long time." He didn't mention gambling, since it was a sore subject, but he took pride in his skills.

She didn't say anything, but by looking at her, he could read the thoughts going through her mind.

"I've toyed with the idea of raising horses. I've always had an interest in that—discovering the strength and weaknesses of different breeds. I have friends in Ireland who would help me get started."

"You haven't spoken of this before."

"So far it's just an idea in my head. I haven't talked about it until today."

"You're speaking to *me* about it. Why me, and not Mr. Bunney for instance?"

"You're making complications where there aren't any, Cassie. Perhaps I wanted to share with you because I consider you a friend."

Again an awkward silence grew between them. He

wanted to say she'd become more than a friend. "I trust you, Cassie," he added.

"Thank you."

He waited for her to return the words, but she said nothing. His chest felt heavy. He knew why she didn't trust him and resentment grew within.

"I don't know what I have to do to prove to you I'm trustworthy. I don't believe I have to prove anything."

She shook her head. "No, perhaps not, and I don't see why it matters whether I trust you or not."

He clenched his jaw until it hurt. "No, I suppose it doesn't. You're leaving soon, and from then on you'll be out of my . . . the Wenthaven family. Well, you'll carry the name until you remarry, but—"

"I have no plans to remarry. James took away any pleasure in the idea of marriage." She chewed on her bottom lip, and her forehead creased as if she carried a lot of pain that wanted to come out. She obviously fought her tears, and a wave of tenderness squeezed his heart. James had always been a selfish bastard.

"What did James do to you?" he asked.

She averted her face lest he read her struggle. "James had no respect for anything living. He was a man poor in spirit and rich in pride."

"Amen to that." Dylan touched her shoulder. Tears glittered on her eyelashes. "Did he hurt you?"

"If you call ignoring my existence a hurt, then yes, he did, but he never touched me with the aim to inflict pain. Still, without love, there's pain."

Dylan agreed to that. "You deserved better, Cassie. You deserve the best."

Her face crumpled and tears started running down her face. Feeling her suffering keenly, he pulled her into his arms and held her tightly. She cried silently for a time, her shoulders heaving with the sobs. He inhaled the fragrance of her hair, savoring every moment.

He could hold her forever and not get tired of her. How unlikely a pair they would be, or—it would never happen. She could never accept his past.

Fifteen

Cassie cried a lot that afternoon. Dylan had dried her tears with his handkerchief. She had read the infinite tenderness in his eyes, and her heart had lodged in her throat. Now she was crying about the past, but not entirely.

She had never felt for anyone what she did for Dylan. He had captured her entire attention, and part of her recoiled in horror that she could be attracted to a Wenthaven man, and a gambler to boot.

It just wouldn't do. She had more control than falling for someone like Dylan Wenthaven. He *did* need her, but for all the wrong reasons. He would have to create his own stability. She couldn't do it for him, nor would she even try.

He wouldn't change. How could he? He knew nothing but gambling for his livelihood.

How could she live with the idea that Fairweather had been restored with gambling money? She certainly couldn't live under the same roof with him knowing the truth.

She dried her eyes, disgusted with herself for her weakness. After washing her face, she went downstairs, hoping no one would notice her swollen eyelids and red nose.

No more had she stepped downstairs before someone knocked on the front door. She heard several loud voices, and she hurried to open the door.

Outside stood four gentlemen, obviously from the metropolis if their clothing was an indication. Their horses had been tied to the trimmed shrubs along the front, which annoyed her because the plantings were in bloom.

"Madam, we're looking for Dylan Wenthaven. This is Fairweather, isn't it?"

She only nodded, suspicious now as the young man grinned with practiced charm. He wore his blond hair in the latest curls, and his shirtpoints were impossibly high. A corpulent older man wore a coat of the finest cut and many rings on his fingers; the other two had the stamp of elegance in their perfect neckcloths and silk waistcoats. No country squires here.

"Yes, this is Fairweather."

"Let me introduce us," the blond man said. "We're Wenthaven's cronies: Lord Manville"—he gestured to the corpulent man—"the brothers Nelson, and myself, Viscount Henley-Smythe." He peered around the door. "Where is that rogue Wenthaven?"

Everyone in the house must have heard the commotion because they came to the hallway and greeted the strangers. Mr. Bunney came out with both his arms in matching silk slings.

"Percy! Lucius, Harry, and Reggie!" He surged forward as everyone watched. "Come in, come in," he exclaimed.

Dylan arrived shortly afterward from the stables and greeted his friends with hearty handshakes. Everyone was talking at once, giving Cassie a headache. Dylan threw her a searching glance. She avoided his eyes. Though she could feel his concern across the room, she pushed it away.

"Wenthaven, we've traveled all day. A bottle of brandy wouldn't come amiss, y'know," said the blond man, Percy. "We never thought we'd find you here, hiding away as you are."

"I'm not hiding," Dylan protested, looking sheepish. "I'm seeing to my property, however pitiful it is at the moment."

He invited everyone inside, and the men repaired to the dining room to have their brandy and talk. It was the only room that had a group of chairs.

For some reason, Cassie felt uneasy. Dylan's face had lit up when he saw the gentlemen, and she'd never seen him so animated. They reminded him of what he missed in the capital, no doubt.

Perhaps he would drop everything and go back to London. But why would that thought bother her? Within two weeks she would be gone from Fairweather. The mansion's fate was out of her hands now.

Just as she headed toward the kitchen to speak with Mrs. Granger, there came another knock on the door. This time, the local constable, Mr. Sweeney, stood on the steps outside. A young woman of humble appearance stood beside him. She had a pretty face, and brown ringlets fell over her shoulders. Not more than seventeen years old, Cassie thought, and noted her bulging stomach. Clearly she was increasing.

"Mrs. Wenthaven, I have some news for you. This is Letty Hale—Mrs. Jonathan Hale, from the next village. Can we come in for a moment?"

"Certainly." Cassie held the door wide for them and ushered the young woman to a chair in the foyer.

The constable stood nearby, twirling his hat between his hands.

"I think you should fetch Mr. Wenthaven," the constable said. "I have news that concerns him."

The baby, Cassie thought. This was Christopher's mother, no doubt. And Dylan could be the father.

On trembling legs, she went to the dining room door and called Dylan. Surprised, he rose from the table and joined her in the hallway, closing the door behind him.

Constable Sweeney greeted him apprehensively. "I have unearthed the truth about the young orphan you found on your doorstep," he said. "This is his mother, a barmaid from Peevey, and she has confessed to leaving the baby on your doorstep."

The woman gave Dylan a beseeching glance. "Aye, that I did an' all, but 'twas all in 'ope that ye'd care fer 'im as 'e ought to be cared for. I loved the little tyke, but I can't take care o' 'im. My new 'usband didn't want nothing to do wi' 'im, y'see."

She wrung her hands agitatedly. "Mr. 'Ale didn't want a child born on the wrong side o' the blanket in 'is 'ouse." She looked sad for a moment, then said, "Ye look a bit like yer older brother, Mr. Went'aven. James wus allus kind to me. Gave me trinkets and money when I had nothin'. Then the baby came. I knew 'e would've taken care of me, but 'e died, didn't 'e? So I can't take care of the boy, and it saddens me no end."

Cassie froze. "James is the father of the infant?"

Letty nodded. "Aye. James wus me lover for some time, I'm not ashamed to admit it. 'E would niver marry me, I knew that, seein' as 'e wus already married. But 'e niver wus 'appy wi' 'er."

Dylan glanced at Cassie, and she thought she

would fall through the floor, but nothing happened. James had fathered Christopher. And she'd thought Dylan had acted in some careless fashion. James had not only fathered a child, he'd committed adultery.

The knowledge hurt very much for a short while. Then she took a deep breath, and surprisingly the sense of betrayal went away. Truth was that she'd never loved James. No matter what James had done, Christopher was a blessing.

"Is there any way I can adopt him?" Cassie asked the constable.

He rubbed his head, clearly thinking about possibilities. "I don't know, but if you don't, the boy will end up at the orphanage, and that's the same as the poorhouse."

"That won't happen as long as I am alive," Cassie said.

"I agree with that," Dylan said. "The boy is my nephew; he's a blood tie, and I would like to take care of him."

"You'll have to work that out between you two," the constable said. "Only one party can adopt him."

"Yes," Dylan said, and Cassie felt his searching gaze on her. "We shall talk about it. And the boy stays here for now. I'm pleased the matter is cleared up."

"Aye, so am I," the young woman said, obviously relieved.

"My solicitor will draw up all the necessary papers," Dylan said to her. "All you have to do is sign them."

"Mr. 'Ale will be that 'appy to 'ear it. I've been frettin' over the fate of the tyke, and now I can be at peace." She smiled from ear to ear, and Cassie wondered how she could give her son away. People thought and felt differently.

The constable left with Letty Hale and Cassie sat down on the vacated chair. The men were laughing in the dining room, and she could hear Mr. Bunney drone on about his adventures. The shock of the news felt like a blow to her head.

"We'll have to talk about this, but I fear this is not the time," Dylan said. "I want you to know, though, that the baby will always be able to have a home with me."

"Or with me."

"Or with *us*."

"Us?"

"There's always that possibility, Cassie."

She closed her mouth, which had fallen open in surprise. What was he offering her?

"I'm returning to my friends now. We'll talk later this evening, if you don't mind."

She nodded mutely. Everything was happening at once, making her head spin. The only "us" she could think of was marriage, unless he had in mind some unlikely business partnership. Perhaps he truly wanted her as the steward of Fairweather.

The uncertainty made her feel as if she were teetering on a cliff with a bottomless abyss below. She wanted to pace and wring her hands like some actress on the stage, but decided to go outside and weed the garden. A lot more useful than theatricals, she thought and forced the chaos of her thoughts into submission.

Nothing like simple labor to keep one's mind in order, she told herself as she donned garden gloves and pulled out her bucket of tools.

* * *

Later that day, her mood improved as she tired herself out digging up tough weeds. She pushed aside all thoughts of Dylan and the future until he came outside to inform her that his friends were staying for dinner.

"I hope you don't mind," he said.

"No, why would I mind? They are your friends, and we don't have a lot of social interaction in these parts."

He smiled ruefully. "They are a rather ribald lot, not the kind the vicar would invite for Sunday tea."

"I realize that," she replied with a laugh as she remembered the habitual disapproving looks of the Peevey vicar. "But he's not coming to dinner."

Dylan chuckled. "I'm happy you've regained your sense of humor."

"It was never gone, except that the situations around here haven't inspired humor. Especially the time when we were running around with buckets and pans for the leaks."

He nodded. "Yes, indeed, no laughing matter. But we're not going to have to carry buckets for much longer—only if it rains before the roof is ready."

She straightened her back and pulled off her gardening gloves. Dry dirt fell out of the folds of her skirt. She could sense his gaze intently on her, and she was afraid to look at him.

"What I said earlier—" he began.

"Is there anything to say?" she interrupted hastily.

"Yes, there is." He spoke with conviction and put his hands on her shoulders. She noticed they were shaking.

She stood utterly still. "What—?"

"Cassie . . ." He took a deep breath. "I want to marry you. Will you do me the honor of becoming my wife? Somewhere in these last few weeks, I found I've fallen in love with you."

Stunned, she couldn't find her voice. She swallowed convulsively. "I . . . don't know what to say."

"Just say yes. It's that easy."

She wished she could just throw caution to the winds and agree with him. Her heart was dancing in her chest, but her mind warned her that Dylan had many flaws. She liked him a lot more than she had James, but he was still a Wenthaven.

"No, right now I can't accept. I'm honored, however."

"You're making things difficult, Cassie. If it's my gambling standing in the way, I'll find another source of income. I've found that I can be resourceful."

"The gambling is one thing, but I can't ask you to change for me. I worry about being hurt."

"The difference between me and James is that I love you, Cassie."

And I love you, she thought, but couldn't say it.

"Perhaps I'm asking you too quickly, but ever since I saw you on the landing that first morning when I arrived, I knew you were the woman for me. Not that I could formulate that for myself until just these last days. When I kissed you in the maze, my heart melted. That's the only way I can explain it."

She could dissolve right into his arms, but she braced herself. "I have to think about it, Dylan."

"At least you're calling me by my first name," he said wryly.

She could read the disappointment in his eyes, but she could not give him the answer he wanted. "There's no hurry, is there?"

He shook his head and dropped his arms to his side. "No, there isn't."

Without another word, he turned on his heel and left the garden. She sat down on the wrought-iron bench and looked out over the water. Had it been a mistake to turn him down? Her heart felt heavy, but she couldn't quell the fears brought forth by his proposal. Tears stung her eyes, but would not fall.

Overwhelmed with everything that had happened, she went inside. The best thing to do was to pray over the situation for some clarity.

Sixteen

She spent the rest of the day in solitude and claimed a headache to avoid dinner. Perhaps it was rude to Dylan's friends, but she just couldn't face them after all that had happened.

Feeling poised and purged by her prayers, she decided to have a cup of tea in the kitchen and chat with Mrs. Granger. Some leftovers would appease her hunger.

When she stepped into the hallway, she heard loud male voices coming from the dining room. They all were talking at once and laughing uproariously at someone's joke. She could hear glasses clinking, and expressions of toasts. Just as she passed the dining room door, it opened. Percy came out, reeling from inebriation. He leered at her and was about to say something when Dylan saw her through the open door.

Brandy bottles littered the table and a deck of cards had been dealt. The smoke of cheroots filled the room, and the gentlemen had removed their coats and loosened their cravats. The scene reminded her of the past, when James had spent evenings with his cronies and she'd been admonished to stay away. Not that she'd had the slightest intention of joining them.

Uneasiness rolled through her. Dylan rose from his chair and gave her a warm smile. She wanted to smile back, but couldn't.

Percy exited the house through the front door, brandy fumes wreathing around him. The other gentlemen laughed uproariously at something Mr. Bunney said.

Dylan joined her by the door. "We're enjoying a rubber of whist and good company," he said, his breath laden with brandy fumes.

"I can see that." She hated herself for sounding so stiff.

"It doesn't happen that often," he said, his smile fading.

"Nothing has really changed, has it? This is what you enjoy, and this is what you should continue to do." She condemned harder than the vicar did the sinners in a Sunday sermon.

"I suppose you know best, Cassie," he said and crossed his arms over his chest. He stood square in the doorway, blocking her view. "I hope you're feeling better. How's your headache?"

"I came down to fetch a cup of tea. Where are Hazel and Hermione?"

"They said something about sewing a special coat for Edward due to his difficulty with his arms."

"They would, too. Evidently he has wound them around his finger with his tales of woe."

"Do I detect a note of cynicism in your voice?"

"Let's just say Mr. Bunney has excellent knowledge of how to manipulate people."

"Now I definitely detect cynicism."

"But true nevertheless."

"We all know *you* would never sew a coat for Mr. Bunney."

"My skills with needle and thread are not that advanced. Besides, he has very particular tastes. I wouldn't dream of trying."

"Hmmm, you have a point there. He never scrimps on his tailor's allowance."

"It goes without saying." She went past him toward the kitchen.

"Have you thought about what I offered earlier?" he threw after her.

She hesitated, then turned toward him slowly. "The answer will have to be no, Dylan. I'm sorry."

Every last vestige of his smile disappeared. He closed his eyes for a moment and his face looked drawn. "Very well, Cassie. I accept that, and I shan't pester you with questions of that nature again."

She fled to the kitchen, her heart hammering in her chest. How uncomfortable she had become here. She felt as if she had nowhere to turn now.

The raucous laughter of the gentlemen followed her into the kitchen, and she abhorred it. Dylan wouldn't change.

Dylan looked after Cassie as she hurried away, admiring her slim straight back and the gentle sway of her hips. He had a wild longing to sweep her into his arms and just hold her tightly.

Total helplessness was a feeling he didn't know how to handle. Falling in love had brought more pain to his life than he'd ever thought possible. He understood Eddie's misery now. There was nothing worse than unrequited love. He just wanted to free himself from its snare, but felt helpless about how to do it.

"Blast and damn!" he swore under his breath. He

slammed the door and went back into the dining room. Before the appearance of Cassie tonight, he'd been enjoying himself. Nothing better than to share good conversation and a bottle of brandy with his cronies, especially after a long time without. Nothing wrong in that, surely.

He shuffled the cards and tossed out another hand.

"Looks as if Dylan ate a lemon," Reggie said as Percy reeled back into the room.

"That sister-in-law is a Friday-faced puss, isn't she?" Percy commented. "The sort who could've clouted me with an umbrella and shaken her Bible at me."

"Cassie is wonderful," Dylan defended her, "and if you don't want to taste my ire, you'd better keep your comments to yourself."

"Listen to him!" Reggie chided. "He's like a bull with a sore head."

Dylan pushed his chair back. "If you want to provoke my ire, just fight me. Fight!" This whole experience felt hollow. He looked at his friends through the haze of brandy fumes. He was tired. He'd never drunk much, only on occasion, but he knew he could never convince Cassie of that.

"Blast it, Dylan, I'm only jesting," Reggie said.

"I think Dylan has been struck with Cupid's arrow," Eddie said shrewdly and tossed down his cards from one of the hands trapped in the sling. "I think there's a danger here at Fairweather. If you stay long enough, Cupid will strike you, too."

"I say! There's no worse fate," Harry said, his face twisting in disgust. "I'm never going to wake up beside some prune-faced wife if I can help it."

"Neither am I," Lucius said. "Just imagine: no opera dancers, no courtesans, no flower girls. Life would turn into a rut of drudgery."

"You speak as a man who has never been in love," Eddie exclaimed. "When you're in the throes of passion, you can neither eat nor sleep. You're thinking of nothing else but your beloved. It's a great sickness of the heart, especially since you have no outlet for the wild emotions surging in your chest. 'Twould be almost more merciful to throw oneself over the cliff into the sea."

Dylan agreed wholeheartedly with everything, but said nothing.

"Or maybe shoot oneself through the heart," Eddie continued.

"Very uncouth," Percy said.

"Why would you want to leave such a mess for someone to clean up? 'Twould be very selfish of you," Harry said. "Also, how are you going to shoot yourself with two arms in slings? 'Twould be a very awkward affair."

"Oh, I could find a way," Eddie said breezily.

"We can abduct your lady for you," Reggie suggested and drank deeply from his glass. "And take her to Gretna Green. Her father would never be the wiser until the deed was done."

"By Jove, 'tis an idea that warms my heart, but I have to disagree," Eddie replied and burped. "I have a hankering for gaining her hand through honest means."

"After what you told us, 'twill never happen," Reggie said. "Mr. Duggan seems rather set in his ways."

"That's putting it mildly." Dylan snorted.

"We've had nothing but hardships from him," Eddie said, his expression pained. "My arms ache like the devil, and I have to drink brandy to keep the fangs of pain at bay. I declare, my arm will rot away with poison in the wound."

"Rubbish," Dylan replied. "I saw Ripple cleaning that wound thoroughly and spreading basilicum powder on it. You'll be right as rain in a fortnight."

"Listen to Dylan," Eddie said peevishly. "This is the kind of treatment I've been submitted to since I arrived. No understanding, no coddling."

"You've had nothing but from everyone, especially from the elderly twins. What you haven't had available is your usual adoring court from London."

"I have given up everything for love."

Dylan could barely keep himself from delivering a sharp comment.

"Then you'll have to succeed, since there's nothing else," Reggie said. "You need our help."

"You helping Eddie will only make matters worse," Dylan said. "You don't know Duggan. If he thinks you're a threat to his family and peace of mind, he won't hesitate to shoot you. He has that volatile a temper."

"Such a challenge never bothered me," Reggie said, fiddling with the stem of his brandy snifter. "I'm ready for an adventure."

"I won't allow you to stir up a conflict here," Dylan said.

"Listen to him," Percy exclaimed. "He sounds like a stodgy squire. Where's your sense of adventure, Wenthaven? You never shied away from a lark."

"This is different, Percy. I have to live here, whereas you can leave any kind of havoc you create behind."

"He has a point," Eddie said. "I don't want to cause any trouble. I will have to carry my pain without complaint."

"That's very heroic," Harry said, and lit another cheroot. "You are showing a side we never knew you had, Eddie."

"We're all familiar with your selfish side," Reggie continued in the vein of Harry's observation.

Eddie's eyes grew wide and wounded. "Selfish? I beg your pardon." His voice dripped with injury. "I *never* speak of myself, nor do I put myself forward in any way."

"Only always," Harry corrected him, "but I'm still fond of you. Life would be boring without the Eddies of this world."

"That perception is great injustice and stabs me in the heart," Eddie said, his face reddening.

"I have no fear you will challenge me to a fight," Harry said, laughing.

"You're taking the opportunity to be cruel and callous," Eddie said, anger blazing. "Just wait until my arms are back to normal."

"Unless the one rots and falls off," Reggie teased.

"You shall be my second challenge," Eddie cried. "I never knew my friends to be so cruel!"

"It's time to finish this before someone gets injured," Dylan said. He turned to Eddie. "You'll just have to accept the fact that Duggan won't give you his daughter's hand in marriage."

"Hah! Just because you can't have the lady who has stolen your heart doesn't mean I can't. I won't give up that easily, and I don't think you should, either."

"In my case it would be detrimental to push."

"You never know. Females like to be swept off their feet."

Dylan experienced another wave of helplessness.

He'd never had problems with women in the past, but then he'd never been truly in love.

"Write her a love poem," Harry suggested. "We can help you if your poetic vein runs thin."

"Yes! Let's do that to help Wenthaven," Percy exclaimed. "We have to use words like 'rosebuds,' 'tenderness,' 'delicious doe's eyes,' and the like."

"Delicious doe's eyes? Thunder and turf, you must have windmills in your head, Percy, or you're so drunk you're beyond reasoning," Lucius said, and delicately patted his thinning curls to feel if they still lay in perfect order.

"A poem might not be a bad idea," Dylan said, his mind already turning. "Cassie likes to read. She's forever with her nose in some book she rooted out of the attic."

"We have to use the word 'treasures,' " Percy continued.

"I pray you're not alluding to her bosom," Eddie said, his expression aghast.

Percy moved in his chair and reached for the bottle to refill his glass. "It wouldn't be wholly an untruth," he said. "From what I could see—"

"Desist!" Dylan barked.

"You're as touchy as if the woman were your wife, which she ain't," Percy said sourly.

"If we're writing a poem, it has to be in good taste. My marital status has nothing to do with it. Brown eyes . . . smile of beauty," Dylan mused aloud. "I shall return with pen and paper, and you shall help me. Poetry never was my strong suit." When he came back, the men had thrown themselves wholeheartedly into the exercise.

"Milky white skin," Eddie called out, "eyes of love, brown velvet softness caressing—"

"That's ridiculous, Eddie," Harry blurted out. "How can brown velvet softness caress? Be realistic."

"Molten love," Eddie continued, lost in his own feelings.

"I want to say I believe in Cassie, and nothing that happened in the past has to destroy future happiness for us."

"Well, start 'I believe in you,' " Percy urged.

After lots of arguments and false starts, they had created a poem that struck just the right tone without being banal. Dylan ruthlessly edited out suggestions of "rosebud mouth so sweet," and "eyes of heavenly bliss." He put down his pen and lifted up the piece of paper on which he'd worked. It had many ink blotches, but he could rewrite the poem before giving it to Cassie. Everyone listened intently as he read aloud:

> *I believe in you*
> *In my heart I know*
> *you are good, gentle, and kind*
> *and a lover of truth*
>
> *I believe in who you are*
> *light and love and spirit*
> *molded to perfection*
> *with voice of silver*
> *and smile of joy*
>
> *I believe in your soothing touch*
> *so sweet, so right*
> *awareness mingling freely*
> *with energy sparkling*
> *stars falling*
> *into the everlasting now*

> *As your soul touches mine*
> *I believe in trusting you*
> *as trust heals,*
> *a vigorous climbing rose*
> *that beautifies*
> *the crumbling walls of the past*
> *into a thing of beauty.*

"That's a splendid poem!" Eddie cried. "If her heart remains untouched after that, it is made of rock."

"I never knew we had this kind of talent among us," Harry said. "We've never been challenged thus before."

"And we didn't use any allusion to brown velvet," Percy said proudly.

"I personally think we should have included some suggestion of hair like molten amber," Reggie said. "We didn't mention her hair. Women are very particular about their tresses."

"Her hair is not like molten amber," Eddie exclaimed. "Cassie's hair is brown."

"Perhaps something soft as moleskin," Reggie continued.

"You must be three sheets to the wind, Reg. No woman wants her hair compared to moleskin," Harry cried.

"Moleskin is very soft," Reggie protested lamely.

"Now we're going to write a poem to my Beloved," Eddie said. " 'Tis the least you can do, seeing as I'm so crippled that I can't even hold a goose quill. And mind your spelling."

They spent another two hours composing a poem to Miss Duggan, and because Eddie had the last say about the contents, there were references to "hair like

spun gold," and a "smile brighter than the brightest
star."

Dylan had no idea if it would make an impact on
the young lady's heart, but he hoped so for his
friend's sake. Perhaps Miss Duggan would at least
feel some pity for Eddie's plight.

I can't wait to put this under Cassie's door, Dylan
thought. It would have to work in his favor.

Seventeen

The poem did in fact melt the barriers Cassie had raised around her heart. That Dylan would make the effort to produce a poem especially for her surprised her. She felt keenly the sincerity behind it.

She read it again and cried a little, easing her tensions. Life had not been the same since Dylan returned to Fairweather. It would never be the same.

She decided to go downstairs and search him out, even though the hour was late. When she got to the hallway, she heard snoring in the dining room. Someone had fallen asleep with their face in a brandy snifter, she thought. She decided she didn't want to know who it was.

As she turned to go back upstairs, that cold whirlwind that had touched her before in the same spot appeared suddenly. Unprepared, she felt a rise of panic, but forced herself to relax with a series of deep breaths. This time she would find out what the captain wanted.

"Show me," she whispered, bracing herself, "what it is you want me to know."

The cold air tugged at her, urging her slowly across the floor toward the library. She'd had a strong impression in the past that something might be hidden in the study, but she'd gone over everything so many times that it wasn't possible to find anything new. Or was it? Had she missed something?

She opened the door and lit a candle, placing it on the last damaged chair. It threw eerie shadows across the walls. She thought she saw another person's shadow besides her own, but she was alone, except for the pirate captain's ghost.

"This is ridiculous," she said to the empty room.

Startled, she heard the sound of a deep sigh right next to her left ear. She jumped away, but saw no one. Trembling now, she braced herself and tried to control her fears. The ghost meant her no harm, she knew that.

"What am I looking for? The treasure?"

The air grew colder, and something blew at her neck so that her hairs lifted. She moved forward, and the cold air kept coming in gusts. She found herself standing in front of the bookcase, where she'd stood so many times before looking for clues.

"Is this the spot?" she asked, and freezing air enveloped her in what she could only believe was a hug.

She knew without any doubt something had been hidden in the bookcase. But where?

An urge to pull down all the books came over her. She hadn't noticed anything when she'd put them back after the break-in, but there was always the slightest chance she'd missed something.

She started stacking the books on the floor and the musty odor of moldy pages filled her nose. Would there be something hidden inside one of them? She hoped not. She didn't feel like going through them.

"Is the key in one of these?" she asked the air,

but didn't feel any kind of confirmation. She would just trust her sensations.

Nothing happened until she'd removed all of the books and was staring at the bare shelves. Then the air grew still colder and anticipation began filling the room. It was as if the ghost were holding its breath, and she as well.

"It's inside somehow, isn't it? Behind the wood?"

The words rang true. She got the only chair left in the room, and put the candlestick on the floor. Getting up on the chair turned out to be somewhat precarious, but she managed to balance herself and look at the shelves from above.

Nothing much of interest struck her, but she noticed a knot in the wood that had somehow swelled out of the shelf. It looked like a flaw in the craftsmanship, but it didn't seem to fit. The rest of the bookcase had been crafted with great care.

She pushed it down and found that it moved. As she watched in amazement, the entire structure of the shelves started moving outward with a groan, almost knocking her over.

As she jumped off the chair, the shelves came to a stop and she noted a huge spring inside that evidently had been maneuvered as she pushed the knot in the wood. Behind the shelves was a black hole.

As she raised the candlestick to glance inside, her heart hammered with anticipation. The door opened behind her, and she whirled around. Dylan stood on the threshold, his cravat askew and his shirtsleeves rolled up. His undress was unacceptable in polite circles, but that thought was a fleeting one. Besides, they were hardly in the thick of society at Fairweather, though she had to admit more people had visited in the last few weeks than had in the entire time she'd lived here.

"What are you doing, Cassie? I heard a groaning noise and came to investigate."

He saw the hole in the wall and his eyes narrowed. "I say. How did you figure this out?"

She couldn't tell him about the ghost. "I had a . . . a feeling I missed something in here." It wasn't entirely an untruth.

"Have you looked inside?"

She shook her head, and he took the candlestick from her. Brandy fumes hung heavy around him, and she was surprised he could walk without weaving.

Together they looked into the opening. At first it appeared there was nothing inside, but as their eyesight adjusted, they found a tall narrow chest that looked very old. It had the ornate baroque ornamentation of the seventeenth century, and Cassie would bet the lock and the hinges were of gold. They gleamed a warm yellow despite spending a long time hidden behind a false wall.

"There truly is a treasure," Dylan said, clearly breathless with surprise. "It wasn't just a cruel joke."

"No." She turned the key in the lock, and it budged without a problem.

He helped her open the domed lid. Underneath they saw fabric, beautifully loomed brocades in yellow and white. Beneath those, as they lifted them carefully, lay a stack of masks, Egyptian in style, which she recognized from paintings she'd once seen in London at an exhibit. These were ancient masks, from the time of the pharaohs.

"So like those I found in Mr. Duggan's study," she whispered. "These are the masks he was looking for. Somehow he knows about them, but would not share the knowledge lest we find them first. It's my guess Captain Brooks stole these from Duggan's ancestor—killed him over them."

" 'Tis a sad possibility. We will never know the truth, but I believe you're right."

"Dylan, do you believe Mr. Duggan would have *real* masks in his study? They must be worth a fortune."

Dylan turned one over and looked at the perfectly crafted gold and lapis lazuli. "Priceless, I'd say. These should be in a museum, not in someone's study. Mr. Duggan is a fool if he thinks he alone has a right to these."

She nodded in agreement. "What else is inside?"

They carefully removed the masks and put them on the desk, all four of them. Below the masks they found more fabric, this time crumbling red velvet. It covered something hard and pebbly, and when Cassie lifted the cloth, they found the glitter of many gold coins.

Dylan whistled under his breath. "This is beyond strange, wouldn't you say?"

Cassie had to agree. "These are gold doubloons."

Dylan dug into the glittering gold and studied some of the imprints. "Ducats also. My ancestor surely conquered some foreign vessels."

Cassie looked at Dylan and he looked at her. "You're thinking my thoughts," he said. "This will more than amply provide for the restoration of Fairweather. These coins are worth a lot these days, not to mention just the weight of the pure gold."

"This is too uncanny. Just as we need the funds the most, we find them from another era. It was as if Captain Brooks provided for the future without any inkling of what was to come."

"Crassly enough, I believe he provided for himself and his just in case hardships would fall upon them," Dylan said, sifting through the trunk. "All money."

"You're probably right about the captain's selfish motives." Cassie wondered if the ghost would acknowledge that. Nothing had happened since Dylan entered the room, but when she walked over to the desk, she felt that distinct whirlwind of cold air.

She whispered, "These are more important to you than the coins, aren't they?"

Again she felt that strange confirmation, an icy hug.

"I believe these belong to the Duggan family," she said, and that ghostly feeling overcame her so strongly that goosebumps rose on her skin.

"As I said, they belong in a museum, but truly they belong to the Egyptian people," Dylan said. "We ought to talk to Mr. Duggan about this and settle the matter forever."

Dylan nodded. "I'll write a note and have it sent over with Ned. Even if we have to rouse Duggan out of his slumber, he won't mind."

"I'm sure you're right."

Half an hour later they heard Mr. Duggan's loud voice in the foyer. He sounded terribly upset and Ned Biggins kept telling him he knew nothing about the matter.

Mr. Duggan's booming voice could wake the dead, and Cassie soon found he'd just done that as four deadly drunk gentlemen, groggy and unsteady on their legs, rolled into the room on Duggan's heels, one carrying a fireplace poker and another a candelabra as weapons. A third brandished a pistol. Mr. Bunney carried only his arms in the slings.

"What is going on here?" Mr. Duggan demanded.

"Is there a battle under way?" the man named Percy slurred and leaned against the wall.

"Mr. Duggan, I'm glad you could join us. We have something to show you," Dylan said.

Before anyone could move, Mr. Duggan had seen the masks and hurried across the floor. He stood in silent awe over them, gently touching the contours of one particularly beautiful mask.

"They were burial masks that they put on the mummies," Duggan explained. He looked at Dylan, calculation filling his eyes. "They are mine."

"That depends. They were found here on Fairweather," Dylan said. "Among Captain Brooks's things."

"Be that as it may, my ancestor was killed because of these, and I have a written account to prove it."

"You were trying to take them by stealth," Dylan continued. "You had people break in here to find them."

"You have to remember that *your* ancestor committed a crime against mine."

"You still broke in, acting in complete disregard for our privacy and frightening the ladies." Dylan's voice held a hard edge. "Constable Sweeney knows all about it, and I can always involve Bow Street if need be."

"These are mine," Duggan said obstinately.

"I could stake a fortune on the fact that the Egyptian people would have a different opinion. In fact, under British law there might be some clause that would prevent you from keeping historical artifacts in your private collection."

"Balderdash!"

"I shall have my solicitor look into the matter," Dylan said. "You haven't heard the last of this."

Mr. Duggan caressed the masks as if they were alive and precious beyond anything else. "What a civilization."

"I'd like to settle the feud once and for all," Dylan continued.

"What do you want in return?" Mr. Duggan asked slyly.

Dylan rubbed his jaw and looked at his friends, who stood in a half circle around Mr. Duggan as if ready to protect Fairweather against this monster.

His gaze landed on Mr. Bunney, Cassie noticed, and she knew what he was going to say before he spoke.

"Mr. Duggan, the masks are yours under two conditions: one, you have a special codicil put in your will that the masks will go to a museum after your demise. As it is, you don't need the funds that the masks might bring in. Number two: You give your permission to Mr. Bunney to court your daughter. I can vouch for him. He's a good man, and he truly loves Giselle."

Mr. Duggan looked as if he wanted to punch Dylan. "No terms!"

"Then the masks won't leave Fairweather. We'll fight you to the last man," Dylan said.

Cassie had never seen him so forceful.

Mr. Duggan thought for a time that seemed an eternity. He could not take his eyes off the masks. "Very well. I agree."

"And no more feuding. Fairweather will be rebuilt, and you'll just have to accept the fact it'll never be yours."

Mr. Duggan nodded. "That's not a problem. It's the dilapidated state that bothers me."

"Then take the masks, and not a word will be

spread from here. These men would never betray me," Dylan said of his friends. "And expect Mr. Bunney to call on Giselle tomorrow morning at eleven. If Giselle loves him, then the match should be sealed with nuptials."

Mr. Duggan nodded with difficulty. He gave Mr. Bunney a sullen look, but there was surrender in every line of his body. He gingerly wrapped the masks in the old brocade that ripped even as he touched it, but he didn't seem to notice.

For a moment, there was total silence. Then the window flew open and a wind whined through the room and blew outside. Cassie wondered if anyone noticed the wind had traveled in the wrong direction.

When Mr. Duggan had left, Dylan showed his cronies the gold treasure. They stood in quiet admiration.

"Dylan, you lucky dog. Who but you would find a hidden treasure that will take care of your entire future?" Mr. Bunney said.

Dylan placed his arm around Cassie's shoulders. "I didn't find it, Cassie did. Only because she believed an old ghost story about a hidden treasure."

The men looked at each other. "Let's finish that brandy," Percy suggested.

The men trooped outside, and closed the door.

Dylan didn't remove his arm. He turned Cassie toward him and raised her chin with his index finger. He kissed her lightly on the lips. "I love you, Cassie, more than you'll ever know."

"I know. Your poem touched my heart, and broke down my defenses. I love you, too." Her heartbeat escalated alarmingly as she realized she'd let down all of her walls.

"No more gambling, Cassie. I promise you. I'll

use some of this treasure to start my horse breeding venture."

"I don't want to start our life together with conditions. I have to trust you, Dylan, and I do. It's all about trust, isn't it? You're nothing like James, and I know your gambling is not an illness. I judged you too harshly in the past."

"So you dare to take the leap with me?"

"Yes, I will take the chance and leap with you into matrimony, Dylan. And we already have a family with little Christopher and the boarders."

"Christopher?"

"That's his name. Don't you like it?"

"I like *you*, Cassie, forever and ever. And you'll have to offer up a public apology when the restoration is done. I remember our wager."

She laughed. "I will pay my stake as promised."

He bent his face to hers. As his kiss touched her soul, Cassie wanted to weep with the beauty of it, and for the feeling of having finally found her harbor.

Captain Brooks looked on from the ceiling. He enjoyed the fact that Fairweather had inspired all these feelings of responsibility and dedication in Dylan Wenthaven, but more than anything he liked to see Cassie happy. She deserved it after all her hardships.

She had managed to find the treasure. The endeavor had worn him out, but he had accomplished his goal. He could go home now, but maybe it wouldn't be wasted time to hang around for a few more years to see the finished result of the restoration. Perhaps he would hear the patter of little feet besides those of baby Christopher. Ugh, what a name! The boy should have been christened something solid like Fortunatus. There was nothing wrong with tradition.

And he would, of course, hang around for the wedding. There was light all around him now, and he could spread some of that in his protégé's life, especially for the wedding. Hmmm, he had work to do.

Flower petals would be good. He'd work up a good wind to spread some flower petals for the nuptials.

More Zebra Regency Romances

__A Taste for Love by Donna Bell $4.99US/$6.50CAN
    0-8217-6104-8

__An Unlikely Father by Lynn Collum $4.99US/$6.99CAN
    0-8217-6418-7

__An Unexpected Husband by Jo Ann Ferguson $4.99US/$6.99CAN
    0-8217-6481-0

__Wedding Ghost by Cindy Holbrook $4.99US/$6.50CAN
    0-8217-6217-6

__Lady Diana's Darlings by Kate Huntington $4.99US/$6.99CAN
    0-8217-6655-4

__A London Flirtation by Valerie King $4.99US/$6.99CAN
    0-8217-6535-3

__Lord Langdon's Tutor by Laura Paquet $4.99US/$6.99CAN
    0-8217-6675-9

__Lord Mumford's Minx by Debbie Raleigh $4.99US/$6.99CAN
    0-8217-6673-2

__Lady Serena's Surrender by Jeanne Savery $4.99US/$6.99CAN
    0-8217-6607-4

__A Dangerous Dalliance by Regina Scott $4.99US/$6.99CAN
    0-8217-6609-0

__Lady May's Folly by Donna Simpson $4.99US/$6.99CAN
    0-8217-6805-0

Call toll free **1-888-345-BOOK** to order by phone or use this coupon to order by mail.

Name_____

Address_____

City_____ State_____ Zip_____

Please send me the books I have checked above.

I am enclosing $_____
Plus postage and handling* $_____
Sales tax (in New York and Tennessee only) $_____
Total amount enclosed $_____

*Add $2.50 for the first book and $.50 for each additional book.
Send check or money order (no cash or CODs) to:
Kensington Publishing Corp., 850 Third Avenue, New York, NY 10022
Prices and numbers subject to change without notice.
All orders subject to availability.

Check out our website at **www.kensingtonbooks.com**.